SPECIAL MESSAGE TO READERS

This book is published under the auspices of

THE ULVERSCROFT FOUNDATION

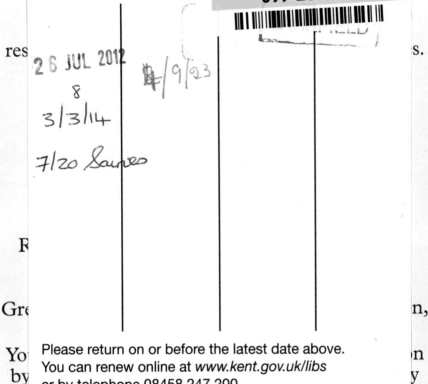

THE ULVERSCROFT FOUNDATION,
c/o The Royal Australian and New Zealand
College of Ophthalmologists,
94-98 Chalmers Street, Surry Hills,
N.S.W. 2010, Australia

TURN OF THE TIDE

It's the 1970s, in the coastal town of Longsands. Tim is easy-going and contented, but Katie wants to move up in the world and she refuses to be thwarted in her desire. Needing to find money to fund the first steps on the property ladder, her drastic solution rebounds on her with devastating effects ... Meanwhile, Gordon and Maureen, with their small baby, move to the affluent area of the South Coast town, when Gordon's firm relocates from London. Four people, who together, will soon find their loves and lives turned upside down ...

Books by Joan M. Moules
Published by The House of Ulverscroft:

SCRIPT FOR MURDER

JOAN M. MOULES

---------------◆---------------

TURN OF
THE TIDE

Complete and Unabridged

ULVERSCROFT
Leicester

First published in Great Britain in 2011 by
Robert Hale Limited
London

First Large Print Edition
published 2012
by arrangement with
Robert Hale Limited
London

The moral right of the author has been asserted

British Library CIP Data

Moules, Joan.
  Turn of the tide.
  1. Large type books.
  I. Title
  823.9'2–dc23

  ISBN 978–1–4448–1176–6

Published by
F. A. Thorpe (Publishing)
Anstey, Leicestershire

Set by Words & Graphics Ltd.
Anstey, Leicestershire
Printed and bound in Great Britain by
T. J. International Ltd., Padstow, Cornwall

This book is printed on acid-free paper

For Joyce and Terry with love

Prologue

There is a tide in the affairs of women,
Which, taken at the flood, leads — God
knows where.

BYRON

Katie grew up watching the tides. They fascinated her. The regularity of them giving a rhythm to everything. She loved walking along the seafront at Longsands when the tide was out. She used to stand by the railings and gaze at the expanse of sand that stretched before her, and at the glimpse of the sea in the distance. She could never decide which she enjoyed most; that picture postcard view which always looked calm, or high tide when the water covered the sand and splashed over the pebbles below the promenade.

She loved watching the colours of the sea too, never knowing which of those she liked best. They continually surprised her as they changed from grey, green, blue, turquoise, mauve and purple. Often streaks of all the colours in the universe seemed to be mixed together in the shades of the sea. The glow of the setting sun which turned the water pink

1

and orange, the ethereal light of the moon which gave it a serenity and gentleness. It soothed her when she was sad or worried and it excited her when it was a rough, angry beast, hitting the shoreline and throwing its powerful anger in great sprays across the esplanade. These days she often wished she could harness some of its vitality into their lives, hers and Tim's . . .

Part 1

1

Longsands, Sussex. Mid 1970s

'You'll never be anything more than you are now. You don't even try to get out of the rut, or whatever it is we've lived in for the last five years . . . '

'Katie, be fair, there's no other work in this town. It's not my fault the wages are so low. If I ask for more I'll be out on my ear, you know that as well as I do.'

Katherine Bray tossed back her vigorous dark hair and walked from the room. In the tiny kitchen she filled the kettle, banging it against the sink in her anger. Taking two mugs from the hooks beneath the shelf she gave them similar treatment as Tim walked through.

Encircling her waist, he twisted her round to face him. 'Five years ago you were thrilled with this place. 'We'll make it cosy,' you said, and we have . . . '

'Five years ago, yes. But I never thought to still be here. Look at it. Oh we made it cosy, after a fashion, but we never stopped the water running down the walls, or the draught whistling up the stairs every time someone opens the front door . . . '

'Listen I'm not working tonight. How about we go out for fish and chips.'

'Fish and chips, fish and chips — can't you ever rise above fish and chips?' Roughly she pushed him from her and concentrated on the kettle now filling the tiny room with steam.

'I don't want to go out for fish and chips. I want a better place to live, a house of our own, a place that is private without others up and down the stairs all day and night. A place that is dry, and warm in the winter, a house with space and cupboards, a garden, oh God — ' She turned quickly, replacing the kettle and fumbling for the teapot lid.

Five minutes later, sitting side by side with their mugs of tea she said quietly, 'I'm sorry, blowing my top like that . . . '

Tim's free hand felt for hers. 'It's all right, love. Listen, I'll go down the job centre tomorrow and see if there's anything else. You never know, something better might come up, but meanwhile, a job's a job. It's not too bad, really.'

She took a great swallow of tea. 'I hate being poor, Tim. I suppose that's at the bottom of it. I guess nobody likes being poor but some people cope with it better — you do for instance.'

'Hey, steady on, I don't like it any more than you do but — '

'Tim, we're young, healthy, we've got a lot going for us. I want us to have enough cash now to do some of the things we want to. Holidays and . . . '

'You make us sound poverty stricken. If you want a holiday you can have one. You could go to that schoolfriend of yours for the weekend when I'm working. She's always asking you. The one with the swimming pool in her garden.'

'And what's wrong with a swimming pool in your garden? If I had the money I'd have one, and a sauna, and a tennis court.'

'Well why don't you do that, it'll be a break.'

'No, Tim, no, no, no.'

'Why ever not?'

'Because I'm not visiting Sandra until I have, or could have as much as she has.'

Tim laughed indulgently. 'We'll all be in wheelchairs when that day comes, if it ever does.'

'That's the trouble with you, you'd settle for anything. If you'd stuck it out at nightschool years ago you'd probably be a chef now instead of a washer-up and general factotum, but no, the first dead-end job you got — '

'A lot of millionaires have worked their way up from kitchen boy . . . '

His cheeky grin disappeared as Katie stood up and pushed back her chair. 'By having some get up and go, that's how. By learning everything they could and using the knowledge to better themselves. You don't even get your tips when you're helping out doing waiting service. I wouldn't put up with that system. It's why I left that restaurant where I was working last year; because they started pooling the tips and I was earning more than the others. You've got to fight for what you want in this world, Tim, and sometimes it seems to me I have to do the fighting for us both.'

Later that night, with Tim's arm round her in the double bed, the only new item they had bought when they married, she looked at the crescent moon through the gap in the curtains that he liked to have partly open when they were in bed.

'It's silly I know,' he'd confessed that first night, 'but I hate them completely pulled across. A legacy from my childhood I expect — I always was afraid of the dark when I was small.'

He was asleep now, his hair, several shades lighter than hers, in sweaty curls over his head. Easing herself from his embrace she

8

rolled further over to her side of the mattress but she couldn't sleep. She closed her eyes and let her thoughts drift backwards to the beginning of their marriage. Tim was as gentle with her now as he was then. I suppose I've always been the aggressor, she thought, but a loving one. I've tried to improve things for us both. She smiled to herself as she relived some of those early days.

It had been fun, finding this flat, small, inconvenient, often noisy, with other tenants coming and going all the time it seemed. But it was theirs as long as they paid the rent. She scoured the once-a-month market for the cheapest and cheeriest material she could find and made curtains and cushions. The three small rooms on the middle floor soon began to look less dingy.

For the first six months life had been heavenly and the nights were something to look forward to throughout the drudgery of her job in the basement kitchens of a hotel on the seafront. When had it changed for her? And why? She still loved Tim, physically and mentally, but was she prepared to stay here forever? Surprised to find herself silently crying, she fumbled beneath the pillow for her handkerchief.

Ever since leaving school when she was fifteen, Katie had known what she wanted.

She had seen what it was like for her parents and promised herself it would not be that way for her. She remembered her mother talking about a cottage for her old age, but it never happened. Perhaps Dad was too much like my Tim — or should that be the other way round — she thought now.

Her mind went back further, to life before Tim. Her first job, in a sweetshop, didn't last long, and then the boutique, that had been fun for a while, but it palled. The clothes were expensive but the material was not. Had she been handling some of the lovely silks she had seen in Liberty perhaps she could have made a career in that line. She had been to London only twice in her life and had loved everything about that store, from its architecture to its merchandise. Sometimes she still dreamed of the feel of the materials. She had spent so long in there she even had the very discreet assistant worried. That had made her laugh.

Tim stirred but didn't wake and Katie let her mind wander onto her next job in the jewellers. She had loved that best of all and vowed that one day she would have a few good pieces herself. She had cried when the shop closed down on old Mr Devonshire's death. In her mind's eye she could still see the toffee-nosed nephew who had inherited, and hear his staccato voice saying, 'You haven't been working here long, Miss Arno, and I am sure you will soon find another place.'

He had given her one week's wages and a stark reference that said something like, *Miss Arno worked for my uncle for two months, and appears to have been satisfactory.*

In retrospect she thought she ought to have tried to train for something at that time — instead she found herself a job in the kitchen of one of the hotels for the rest of the summer season. It was meant to be a stopgap while she worked out what she would enjoy training for. There were so many things she would like to do but most of them cost money, which she didn't have.

She had planned on going to night school in the autumn when the hotel job finished. Meanwhile she put her heart and soul into the dreary task of peeling hundreds of potatoes, and washing and drying so much crockery and cutlery that instead of counting sheep at night, she found herself counting plates and knives . . .

It was there, in the dingy basement of the hotel she had met Tim and the die was cast. She fell totally in love and all her plans were put on hold. Hand in hand they used to cross the road to the promenade when they finished at nearly midnight, lean on the railings and let the sea and silence and their closeness wrap them in their own wonderful world. She remembered once saying to Tim as they turned away from the sea and looked across to the facade of the hotel, 'Someday I'm going to walk up the front steps over there and have my food prepared and cooked for me — and the dishes washed up by somebody else afterwards. The contrast between this side and our entrance down those dark, rickety old steps at the back has to be seen to be believed.'

'You have some grand ideas, Katie,' he'd said as he walked her home one night, 'but when you have that determined look in your eyes and that certain tone in your voice, I really believe you will.'

She turned towards him to see if he was laughing at her, but he wasn't.

'We can have anything we want if we work hard enough for it,' she said, and he kissed her and she knew that right now that was all she wanted.

She had been in her final year at school when her mother fell ill. Her father seemed to go to pieces so quickly and in a very short time she found herself looking after them both, organizing the house, shopping and meals. Smiling now through her tears she remembered the night she had gone to a disco with three of her school friends and had fallen asleep. Imagine falling asleep amid all that noise and colour, she thought now, yet, to her great disgust and disappointment, she had. In retrospect it was almost funny, she thought. Lights flashing, loudspeakers blaring out, the thump of the music and the stomping of the dancers' feet. She had rested her chin in her hands for a few seconds to relieve the headache she had felt coming on, and was gone, sound asleep in the midst of the racket.

I saw Mum and Dad die without ever owning anything in the way of property, she thought. Beholden to landlords all their lives. It's not going to happen to us, she vowed silently now.

The front door banged as the people from the upstairs flat returned. She heard the wife shushing her husband, while by her side Tim gently snored. Someday we'll have a place of our own, she told the sleeping man. Someday, somehow, I'll get enough money together to give us a start. The one certain thing I know is that I'm not prepared to stay here much longer. Five years is time enough for improvement.

Rolling back to her husband's side of the bed she kissed him passionately, and he woke, looking startled.

'Katie,' he murmured, as he stretched out his arms and she fitted herself into them, 'Katie, I do love you, darling.'

'I love you too, Tim, more than anyone or anything in the world. I feel awful when I blow my top like I did this evening. I suppose I've always been ambitious, darling. At school I had to be the best — '

Tim laughed, 'You are the best. You don't need to prove it to me.' He snuggled her closer to him but she hardened her heart. If she didn't push him now while they were talking about it, they would be poor and struggling all their lives. She had watched her mother deteriorate to the point of hopelessness; that day she had returned from school to find her laying on the bed with an almost empty pillbox by her side was still vivid in her mind for all that it was so long ago. She could hear her mother's voice whenever she thought about it, 'It was an accident, Katie. I didn't realize I'd taken so many. It was to dull the pain, that's all . . . '

'Tim, let's make a real effort as from this minute. Let's set our sights on being out of this place by the end of the year. If we really put our minds to it we can do it, I know we can. I don't hanker to be a millionaire any more than you do, but we deserve something better than this. It won't just happen, you know, we'll both have to work towards it like mad. Work and save.'

'Of course, darling. I'll be down the job centre as soon as they open tomorrow morning. Katie, oh Katie.'

She moaned ecstatically as his body covered hers. Afterwards Tim went straight to sleep but she lay awake and thought about how lucky they were to have each other. Surely it wasn't too much to expect something more? *It isn't as if we aren't prepared to work for it*, she thought, easing herself from her husband's arms and curling up small. *I'll work every hour there is if I can achieve something and so will Tim. The holiday camp job he landed just after we married wasn't meant to be forever, at least not in my mind . . .*

★ ★ ★

The holiday camp was at the eastern end of the promenade at Longsands. It was a small, family owned and run camp, not in competition with the giants in the larger seaside resorts. Nevertheless they were usually full for the entire season. The staff were expected to turn their hand to everything, if it was necessary. Everything except the entertainment side of things.

She knew Tim preferred the behind the scenes jobs. He isn't a lazy man, she thought now, simply lethargic. She sometimes wondered how hard he would fight if he thought he was losing her. Would he make a showing or would he more or less shrug his shoulders and accept it?

Tim did go to the job centre the following day. 'Nothing for me,' he told her that evening, 'I'm lucky to have a job.'

'That's what they told you, I suppose. Well it's not a good enough job. We'll never save the deposit to put down for a place of our own on what we both earn now. We shall have to find some other way to make money.'

'There is no other way — short of crime.' He laughed nervously. 'You're surely not thinking of robbing a bank, are you, Katie?'

She didn't laugh with him this time. 'Of course not, but I am making you a promise now, Tim. I will be out of here by this time next year, either with or without you.' Her voice was husky with the tears she was holding back.

'If we don't do something about it now, my darling, we'll end up like my mum and dad did. On the middle floor of a dark little house where we can neither see stars nor grass, and paying over the odds for the privilege.'

16

2

A week later, Katie was reading an account of a charity ball, relishing the descriptions of the outfits worn by some of the well known names mentioned, when she caught the smaller headline to the side of the page. *Woman has baby for friend.* Fascinated, she read the column which told the story of two women and an agency.

There are hundreds of women longing for a child and unable to bear one, and there are women who conceive and carry easily. Our aim is to marry the two needs. 'Of course payment is involved, as it is in any business deal, but we operate our agency with responsibility and sensitivity,' the head of the firm was reported as saying.

It wasn't until two days later after a row with Tim, who had sunk back into his, 'well this is our lot and it's not so bad', attitude, that the idea hit her with such force that she knew it must have been buried in her subconscious since she had read the item. With tears of both anger and frustration still glistening in her eyes she rushed into the kitchen and routed through the papers she

kept for potato peelings and other household waste.

It wasn't there. Frantically she ran from the room, down the stairs to the line of dustbins housed in the front area by the railings. Oblivious to the stares of some children playing in the street, she plunged her hands into their bin, eventually finding the paper she needed. She tipped the peelings directly into the bin, replacing the lid crookedly in her haste. With pounding heart, she took the smeared page back to the flat.

Katie re-read the item at least a dozen times, first of all in the bathroom, where she could be utterly private, and later in the kitchen and the bedroom after Tim had gone to work.

How much money? It didn't say. But it was certain to be a lump sum, and a substantial one for such a service, she reasoned.

Could she do it, though? Could she carry a child in her womb for somebody else? Smoothing out and then folding the precious piece of newspaper she put it in her neat brown handbag before walking to work in the newsagent's in the High Street. She enjoyed her job there, even though she was handling very ordinary items and not anything especially beautiful. She loved the social side of it too. Meeting people was so much

pleasanter than being stuck in the basement of a hotel doing menial jobs.

All day as she sold the papers and magazines, reached for the cigarettes and tobacco from the shelf behind her and even read the words of several birthday cards out to a blind man who wanted one for his wife, she thought about the cutting in her bag and wondered what it entailed. Was there a catch somewhere? Only one way to find out, she thought.

That evening before Tim returned from the holiday camp, she had composed a letter to the agency and posted it care of the newspaper where the report had appeared. It was a short letter but a passionate one and she ended it with, *all I ask is an interview. Please grant me that.*

She said nothing about it to Tim. She wanted to but decided that, until she knew more what the advert was about, then least said, soonest mended. They had made up their latest quarrel. These spats never lasted long — we are an attraction of opposites, she thought now. Tim waits to see what happens and accepts whatever turns up, and I try to change a situation. Sometimes I think I could do with a little of his patience and he with some of my . . .

As she heard the front door open and her

husband coming up the stone stairs to their flat, she went into the kitchen to put the kettle on and make him a cup of tea.

★   ★   ★

It was nearly three weeks later when the answer to her letter arrived. For the previous two, Katie had been downstairs waiting for the postman each morning, just in case. She was there that morning too, and she felt herself losing colour as she bent to pick up the buff coloured envelope, the only one lying there. She recognized her own thick, almost strident writing on the envelope, with something like fear in her heart.

Tim was still in bed; he wasn't on duty until later in the morning. Nevertheless she took the letter into the tiny lavatory and locked the door.

It was a bitter letdown. The agency, it said, was closing. They were sorry not to be more helpful and they wished her luck.

Katie ripped the letter in two and immediately realized that it had an address and telephone number on the headed notepaper. She pieced it together and wrote both in her diary. Then she made a pot of tea and took Tim in a cup.

It was a London address and Katie decided

to ignore the message and simply turn up on their doorstep in the hope of finding out something about what was involved. After all, the place wasn't closed yet, the letter only said, *was closing and they couldn't now take on any more clients.* In any case, there were probably other agencies, she thought and it would be stupid not to find out more now she had come this far.

Wednesday was her free afternoon from the shop, and although they didn't close for half-day any longer, they still gave their staff the time off. Katie asked for the following Wednesday morning off too and told Tim she was going to London, 'for a mooch around the shops for the day.'

'Enjoy yourself, love,' he said when he went off to work that morning. 'Do you a power of good, a day out.' She smiled to herself as she recalled his words later when she settled into a seat on the train. Enjoyment wasn't what it was about at this stage. She felt a twinge of guilt in telling a lie, but, until she knew more about it there seemed no point in sparking a possible argument. If it turned out to be a negative journey no harm would be done.

The address she sought was in Paddington and she found it easily. A small brass plate outside the door stated simply *B & B Agency*. Katie hesitated. It looked like one of the many bed and breakfast places in the area but the letter now safely in her neat handbag clearly stated that the B & B stood for Bilton & Bognor, and beneath the heading, in brackets, it said, *Helping you to Motherhood*. Taking a deep breath, she raised her hand and rang the bell.

★　★　★

'And this woman wants a baby so badly that she's willing to pay someone else to have it for her, Tim.'

They were sitting side by side on the settee and he half turned towards her, a look of disbelief on his face.

'But if we had a baby you couldn't sell it.'

'We wouldn't be selling it. It wouldn't be ours. I told you — it would be theirs. The man would father the child but because his wife is unable to carry through a pregnancy, I would carry the child for her.'

'And he — wouldn't touch you?'

Katie tried to keep her voice soft and gentle but it was difficult with the excitement that was rising inside her.

'He wouldn't touch me, Tim darling. I wouldn't even meet him. Not either of them.'

'No, Katie. Every instinct in me says no.'

She bit her lower lip. 'Tim.' Her voice was

very quiet now. 'Tim, can you think of another way we can earn £5,000? Or even half that amount? You can't, can you? This is the answer — as it is their answer too. They have prayed for a baby and they can afford the money. Just think, we shall be helping two people to achieve something that will bring them so much happiness. And ultimately it will bring us happiness too, because it will give us the start we need. With that kind of money we can put a deposit on a house. I don't care how small and grotty it is to begin with because we can make it beautiful, and it will be ours. Oh Tim,' she entwined her arm into his and snuggled close. 'Darling, don't you see how wonderful it could be?'

'No, Katie, I don't. You can't be serious.'

'Yes, I am. I told you weeks ago that I'm not living here for the rest of my life. You may be satisfied but I'm far from it. I love you Tim, I'd never have married you otherwise. I knew you had no money. Neither did I but I thought that together we could change that. I can't do it alone. You won't take a chance on anything, but I will Tim, by God I will. This, this chance — could be our salvation. It will give us a place of our own. Who knows what will happen then. We could do it up and sell it. Remember the old saying, money makes money? All we need is something to begin with. Anyway you won't have to do anything.' Except give your permission, she added silently to herself.

He was quiet for so long she began to be frightened. Was this it? Had she gone too far and was she to lose him after all this? Would he wash his hands of the whole idea?

Suddenly he looked directly at her, fixing his gaze on her eyes. 'You'll want to keep the baby,' he said.

Swallowing with relief she squeezed his hand. 'No. That's part of the agreement I shall sign.'

'You will want to keep it. All women do.'

'I'm not all women.' Now she was angry. 'I shall enter into it as a business proposition. It's the only way. I shall not see the baby nor hold it. Once the child is born my part will be over. Two people will be happy and the baby will have everything it could possibly want, Tim. People who can afford to do this want a child so badly it's bound to be loved. Much more than a haphazard pregnancy that was a mistake. Look at it logically, please, Tim darling.'

'It may not 'take' — this, this procedure you're telling me about. You may not become pregnant.'

'That's true but it's a chance I'm ready to risk. It will be disappointing but we'll be no worse off than we are now. If you don't want to know about it I'll keep quiet until everything is sure.'

'What about other people? What will you tell them? That the baby you are expecting isn't mine and that it will be given away as soon as it's born?'

'Of course not. The less publicity the better I should think. If we say nothing no one will even suspect it isn't yours. Then when the time comes we shall have the money and move. During the interim period we could always say I'd lost the baby.'

'Katie, I don't know.' There was anguish in his voice now. 'Somehow . . . '

'In any case it really is nothing to do with anybody but us. You and me Tim and, and the people who will eventually be the parents.'

'Do you want a baby, Katie?'

His question took her by surprise and for a moment she was silent. Then, looking straight into his eyes she said, 'Not here. There's no room for a baby here. I'm not too bothered anyway, it's you I love. I don't need a child as well. Later, when we've something behind us we can go down that road if we both want to, can't we, Tim?'

3

Maureen Linnet sat in the pleasant kitchen of her modern house in Richley Green, Surrey. Idly she picked up the other paper — Gordon always took the *Telegraph* with him to read during his lunch hour. She poured herself another cup of coffee from the machine bubbling on the ledge and settled down to read the news. She liked to be up to date with both current affairs and the more gossipy bits in the newspaper. She knew that Gordon appreciated this.

'One of the things that never ceases to amaze and delight me', he told her one day, 'is the way you can talk about anything topical, anything at all. Whether it's a world-shattering piece of news or a strange little paragraph about the perplexities of human nature.'

It was quite a small piece that caught her eye that morning. A boxed advertisement printed in heavy type. *Are you longing for a baby? If so, contact us at this number.* On the line below in small print, *This is not an adoption agency.*

Maureen read it again. They had been

through the adoption argument several years before. Yet, if it wasn't adoption, then . . . She walked across to the bureau and wrote the telephone number on the next page of the yellow pad and tore it off. Folding it once she slipped it into the pocket of her skirt. It was Mrs Jones' day so she would wait until the thrice weekly help had gone. After all, she told herself, it couldn't do any harm to find out what it meant.

All morning the thought of the piece of paper in her pocket kept her going. *Are you longing for a baby?* Yes, oh yes, she said silently. Boy or girl, it doesn't matter, but a baby. A child to love and cherish.

When she had married Gordon neither of them realized that she would not conceive. Gordon didn't seem to be worried about it. He had shrugged his shoulders after yet another test she'd had, and said, 'So be it. Some people have children and some don't. We're among the percentage who don't.'

'It's so unfair, Gordon. Look at all the cases you read in the papers. The cruelty that goes on. The people with large families who don't want them and here's us, trying so hard, wanting one so desperately. Just one child, one baby who was ours.' She had once again burst into tears.

The morning seemed to go on forever. She

heard Mrs Jones singing as she went about her work, and she fingered the paper with the telephone number on. Maybe it wasn't anything to be excited about but it seemed so definite in its wording. *Are you longing for a baby, if so contact us . . . .* There seemed no doubt about it and this excited her. After all the years of dashed hopes that advert sounded positive and she responded to its message with all her heart.

'All done. See you Friday, Mrs Linnet.'

'Yes. Thank you, Mrs Jones.'

'I may be a little late on Friday. I have a check-up at the dentist and although I should be out in plenty of time you can't always tell. Sometimes he's running late because something beforehand took longer than the time he allowed. It has happened to me before. I tried for an earlier appointment just in case, but he was full. His snooty receptionist told me, 'It's that one or wait another three weeks', and as you know I shall be on holiday then — '

'Yes, yes, that will be all right. No problem, Mrs Jones,' Maureen was right behind the woman, edging her towards the door. She seemed reluctant to leave this morning and in one of her talkative moods. Sometimes she simply called out, 'I'm off,' and was gone within seconds, and Maureen longed to rush ahead, open the door and push her through. She contained herself of course — good dailies didn't grow on trees and Mrs Jones did her job well.

As soon as Mrs Jones had closed the front door behind her Maureen ran to the telephone. Halfway through dialling the number, panic hit her. What was she doing? What would Gordon say? Maybe she should wait and discuss it with him. But discuss what? Until she telephoned and gathered some information there was nothing she could tell him. Her fingers slipped from the buttons and she became stern with herself. 'Do you want a child or not, Maureen Linnet? If you don't ring this number and find out what it's about you'll regret it all your life.'

Taking a deep breath she tried a third time and was introduced to something she had never in her wildest dreams thought about — surrogacy.

Much later that evening she and Gordon faced each other from the depths of the soft green armchairs.

'Somebody else to carry the child, Maureen, but — '

'We've tried everything else, Gordon. For eight years now I've fought this need in me to have a child. I've filled my life with voluntary

29

hospital work, amateur dramatics, the tennis club, the rambling club, but it's no use. The gap is still there and it's growing worse. So why ever not? This way the baby will be genetically ours — it will be your sperm . . . '

'But — but it isn't natural, Maureen.'

'What's that got to do with it? It will be a baby, our baby.' She couldn't stop the tears and suddenly he was there with his arms about her.

'It — it won't make any difference to our sex life, Gordon; but it will make us a complete family.'

Stroking her face gently he said, 'Listen, I'll think about it. But that's all. I'm not saying I'll agree to this — this scheme.'

'Oh, Gordon.' She raised a tear-streaked face from his shoulder. 'That's all I'm asking right now. For you not to throw the idea out before we've examined it properly.' Her tears wet his face as her lips sought his, and her arms drew him towards her breasts in a passionate embrace.

4

'Suppose she wants to keep it, Gordon. Suppose she won't — or can't part with it when it's born?'

'Of course she will. It's part of the agreement, darling. Anyway it's — it's ours. It's my sperm after all. It will be our baby. Now stop worrying and kiss me. Not like that, Maureen. Properly, as you used to.'

Long after her husband was asleep, his breathing regular and somehow comforting beside her, Maureen thought about the child that had now taken root in someone else's womb. It had not been an easy choice but her overwhelming need for a child had been the decisive factor. For the last eight years she had tried very hard to fill the gap with other pursuits, but it was no use. Nothing answered this hunger in her, this aching hunger for a baby.

When all the tests proved negative — when she had been through the agony of two phantom pregnancies, she had tentatively broached the subject of adoption to Gordon. He wasn't keen.

'We won't know the history, the background . . .'

'If we adopt a very young baby we will shape his or her history, Gordon. We will give the child a stable background.'

'Mmm, inheritance counts for a lot though, Maureen; but if it means so much to you we could think about it . . . '

'Don't you want a child too? Want us to be a complete family?'

'Of course I do, but I also want you. I love you. Sometimes I think you forget that and only think of me as the means of giving you a baby.'

Maureen had sobbed into his arms that night. It was the following day that she had seen the cutting in the paper, rung the number it gave and arranged to go to London for an interview. It seemed like providence to her. Surrogacy. This way it would be Gordon's baby. He would be the biological father. Surely that was the answer if he agreed to do it.

'Five thousand pounds?'

'Oh, Gordon, what does the money matter? We can afford it. There's that money my mother left. Let's use it to have a baby — our baby.'

It had taken time of course. They went to the clinic, answered questions and filled in forms. When they were asked if they wished to meet the potential surrogate they both were certain that they did not. Maureen knew, without him saying anything, that there were moments when Gordon had second thoughts, but she couldn't pull out once she could see there was a chance for them to have a child. Gordon was exceptionally quiet when they returned from the clinic. The only reference he made was to say, almost to himself, 'It isn't natural.'

They heard nothing for several weeks and then they received a letter saying the agency was closing down. Maureen thought Gordon was relieved but she was desperately disappointed. Three weeks later, when she had hit rock bottom she felt so ill and depressed, came a letter from Bilton and Bognor saying that they had taken on another director who had injected some money into the company and it wouldn't be closing down in the foreseeable future. Maureen's heart seemed to be doing strange things as she read on, *We do have someone on our books who would be suitable.*

'It's fate, it's meant to be,' she told herself, but refrained from saying this to her husband.

Two weeks after that came the news that everything was in place to proceed. *All the health tests with our client have proved positive and if you are still of a mind to go ahead please confirm this in writing and we will arrange one more visit for you both to talk to us and ensure this runs smoothly.*

Now they knew it had taken. The woman, this unknown woman who would carry their son or daughter in her womb for nine months had had it confirmed that she was pregnant.

Maureen rocked from one anxiety to the next. Would the baby be healthy? But surely every mother wonders that. Would it look like Gordon? But the greatest of all now the pregnancy was confirmed: Would the woman back down and want to keep the child, their child?

She wanted to ring the agency every day just to make sure everything was all right. She did no such thing of course and somehow she even refrained from talking too much about it to Gordon. Not about the baby but about the means of conceiving it.

They knew nothing about the woman who would carry their child; not her name, nor what part of the country she was from. Only that she was English and had passed all the health tests imposed by the agency.

'That's all we need to know,' she said to Gordon, 'everything else is irrelevant.'

Maureen bought white wool and knitted tiny matinee jackets and bootees. She bought babygros in white and lemon and palest green.

'I don't mind which it is as long as it's all right,' she said to her husband, as mothers have said throughout the ages. She knew that she truly had no preference for boy or girl, simply for a baby. She bought baby magazines and read through the stages of carrying and giving birth, even fancying that her stomach was expanding too as their baby grew. When they had friends round to supper she hid the knitting to avoid awkward questions. They had already decided to say that they were adopting a baby, but not until after the baby was born. Maureen knew that, all being well, they could have their son or daughter home fairly quickly after the birth.

'A week to ten days' the agency had told them when they went for that final meeting. 'Might even be less. Just as soon as it can leave the nursing home.'

'What about feeding?'

'The home will use expressed milk from the mother for the first few days, then they'll put the child onto powdered milk. You will be given details of things like that.'

'The — the woman won't see the child?' Maureen hoped her voice sounded less wobbly to the brisk woman behind the desk than it did to herself.

'No. It will be taken away at birth and looked after in the nursery.'

'Will we be able to visit? Just the baby I mean.'

The official eyes softened for a moment. 'No. It's best this way.' Her voice became quite gentle, 'and it won't be long to wait by then.'

At six months the woman from the agency rang her. Maureen, who was preparing for a dinner party for some of their friends from the tennis club, felt the colour leaving her cheeks when she identified herself.

'Just to tell you that everything is progressing well and the baby should be born around the first week in September, Mrs Linnet.'

When she didn't reply because she was fighting the nausea that had risen in her throat, the voice coming through the telephone earpiece said, 'Mrs Linnet, are you still there? Mrs Linnet?'

'Yes, yes, I'm here. You, you say the baby's all right.'

'As far as we can tell, yes. Just thought you would like to know. I'll be in touch again when the child is born. No complications your end, I take it?'

Recovering her composure Maureen assured her that everything was fine. 'I've stacks of baby clothes, the nursery is ready — '

'Good.' The voice that interrupted her was brisk again. 'Til September then. Goodbye.'

She told Gordon when he came in that evening and they were changing for the dinner party. 'I was so worried when I realized who it was. I thought something had happened to our baby.'

He put his hand beneath her chin and kissed her lightly. 'Silly girl, but my own darling silly girl,' he whispered.

Her only regrets now were that her parents were no longer here and would not get to know their grandchild. Her mother had died just over three years ago, only five months after her husband. It had been a terrible shock for Maureen as they had been to stay with her only the weekend before and she had seemed fine. Looking back now Maureen realized that her passion for a child had become ever more urgent since then. Both she and Gordon had been only children so this baby would have no close relatives on either side; no aunties or uncles to spoil it and no cousins to mingle with. If this worked out well then maybe they could provide the baby with a brother or sister in time. She didn't mention her thoughts on the subject to Gordon. Time enough for that later on when they had their first child with them, she thought, hugging the idea to herself.

The woman from the agency contacted her again when the baby was born. 'A boy,' she said, '8lbs1oz and doing fine. I'll be in touch again in a few days, then I'll be able to tell you when you can have him home. Congratulations, my dear.'

Maureen replaced the telephone receiver and cried. Tears rained down her cheeks and she couldn't prevent them. It's so silly, she thought, because I'm happy. It's wonderful. Our baby has been born. He's here — our little boy. Yet I can't stop crying.

It was nearly twenty minutes later before she had composed herself sufficiently to be able to ring Gordon at his office to tell him the news.

He was home early that evening, with a bunch of red roses for her and a huge blue teddy bear for the baby. 'When do we collect him? When do we see our son, darling?'

'In about a week. She's going to ring again in a few days when everything is settled. Oh, Gordon, I don't know how I'll wait. Now he's here I want him with us,' and she burst into tears again.

They had chosen names several months ago. Jonathan if it was a boy and Judith if it was a girl.

'I shall call him John or Johnnie,' Gordon said. 'Jonathan's such a mouthful and a bit posh sounding too.'

She laughed, 'Jonathan Gordon Linnet. It doesn't sound posh to me, it sounds just great — it flows.'

'I'll ring the shop tomorrow and ask them to deliver the pram,' he said. 'What about nappies?'

'I've done all that. Everything is here except the pram and you know why I wouldn't have that here too soon.'

He smiled at her, 'My superstitious little mother,' he said, kissing her tenderly.

5

'It's a boy. You have a beautiful baby boy, Mrs Bray.' Seconds later he was in her arms and although she hadn't meant to handle the baby at all she felt his warm softness and looked down into two enormous blue eyes gazing at her from a tiny wrinkled face.

'I'm tired, nurse . . . ' Sister appeared then and gently took the baby from her. 'Everything is fine, Mrs Bray. I'll just check on this little fellow.'

Of course the nurse didn't know she wasn't keeping the baby, she thought. You couldn't blame her. It was bad luck that they were suddenly so busy and that Sister had been called away at the crucial time.

He had looked like a tiny old man, all wrinkles and creases, apart from those huge, innocent looking eyes. She had thought babies were born with their eyes shut. Sister was back and they were tidying her up.

'You can have a nice cup of tea when you're back in the ward, and a bit of rest,' she said briskly.

Katie wanted to ask if the baby was healthy but the words wouldn't come and anyway she really was extremely tired.

She returned home the following day and a few days later a cheque for five thousand pounds came through the post. She held it at arm's length. Yes, it was legal: £5,000. Never before had she possessed so much money. Well, she had earned it for a purpose. Now she and Tim could really put down roots. Quickly she dismissed from her mind the visions of country cottages and attractive detached houses with large gardens. This money would enable them to move to a property of their own. A terraced house maybe, possibly one that needed renovating, but one that would eventually be theirs. They had more than enough for the deposit now and this cheque in her hand was the key to better times, even to the saving of their marriage because she wasn't sure they could have gone on as they were for much longer without it breaking down. She shivered. The very thought of her and Tim not being together was awful. Yet others managed with little so why couldn't she? I could, she thought, if there was hope of improving our lot, but it seemed we were stuck there forever and we were already quarrelling far too much, it could only have grown worse as time went on. I couldn't have borne that.

It was a neat house, in the middle of a terrace and on the high pavement which made it a bit of a production getting their furniture in. There were steps either end of the terrace and the day they moved in several children were playing outside. They were skipping and racing up and down the steps, getting in the way of the removal men. Not that there was much furniture, really. Their rented flat had been so small; a table, two chairs, a couple of kitchen stools, the bed, wardrobe and two rather shabby looking armchairs. It was pathetic, she thought and it looked lost in the new house.

Suddenly there were rooms to fill. Two bedrooms, a kitchen/dining room and a front room with a bay window that looked out onto the high pavement. They were all a decent size too, even the bathroom, which she suspected had once been a small bedroom. The house had been built in the 1900s. It was solid, in both appearance and, to her mind, in atmosphere.

'Don't you feel safe here?' she said to Tim that first evening.

'I felt safe before, but if it's what you want . . . ' He glanced round the room. 'Looks a bit bare though, with our few possessions.'

They were in the kitchen washing up, and were surrounded by boxes of personal stuff: photographs, old scrapbooks from her school-days, a few books and some of her mother's pictures. These were mostly country scenes, sheep grazing, horses ploughing a field — large paintings in dark brown frames which her parents had been given as a wedding present from an old aunt. Her mother used to say that they were 'probably worth a bob or two but you can't sell your wedding gifts now, can you?'

'At least they'll fill up the walls a bit,' Tim said now, nodding towards the box containing the pictures. 'Too cumbersome for me, but they'll fit in here all right.'

Katie wasn't too keen on them herself, but had never been able to bring herself to part with them either. Yes, she thought now, they would look good on these walls. She suspected her mother had kept them also because they were so solid and maybe looking at them helped her to dream of living in the country, the one thing she had always wanted to do.

'I don't suppose they're worth much but Mum especially enjoyed them, Tim. They are a bit heavy, I know, but now we've got so much room we'll be able to display them. At least until we can afford something modern.'

They would certainly need more furniture, she thought the next day after Tim had gone to work and she was walking round her domain. They really did have plenty of room now. Why, they might even be able to take a lodger because they would only need one bedroom for themselves.

She had taken three days from her week's holiday for the move and she went out in the afternoon and spent a happy time browsing in the salerooms in the older part of the town. There were several of them, cheek by jowl, and so full of stuff there was hardly room to move around and see it all. Determined to furnish her house with the best stuff she could afford she wandered amongst the mixture of styles in the emporiums. Junk stood side by side with what she would have called quality furniture here. Not that I know much about that, she thought, except for what I like. Maybe that's the best way to start, by buying what I like and learning about it as I go.

Old Mr Pugh, in the largest of the salerooms, watched her carefully, and seeing this, Katie thought it could do no harm to confess her ignorance and make friends with the man.

'I've just moved, to a larger house,' she told him, 'and, while I need more furniture for the place, I also want some good pieces. I haven't a great deal of money at the moment but I'd like to buy the best I can for what I can afford. You obviously know so much about furniture Mr . . . '

'Pugh, George Pugh.' He extended a weather-beaten hand. 'I bin in this business more years than I care to remember. Tell me a bit more about your house. Size of the rooms, height of the ceilings, age of the house . . . '

The afternoon flew by. No one else came into the shop and she finished up drinking a cup of tea with George Pugh, buying a single bed and mattress, a small dressing table and chest of drawers for what she already thought of as 'the lodger's room'.

'Give me the address and I'll deliver it at the weekend,' he said. Her mentor also promised to look out for one or two nice but reasonably priced pieces for her. 'Bide your time, my dear. I know just the sort of things you're after and they'll turn up one of these days. You just pop in and see me once a week and I'll hang on to anything I think will suit you. No problem if you don't have it, but you shall have first refusal.'

★   ★   ★

45

John Smith, who answered her advert in the newsagent's window, turned out to be an earnest looking young man who worked in a local radio and television shop.

'Not behind the counter,' he said, blinking at Katie through his rimless glasses, 'in the repair department.'

'And do you enjoy it?' she asked conversationally.

'Oh, yes, so much, Mrs Bray. One day I shall probably run my own repair business. Repairing and building new sets too.'

'Can you build radios and television sets then?'

'Well, I'm no expert, of course, but I can usually make contact. I built my first radio set when I was ten years old.' He turned away slightly, seeming embarrassed at having talked so much. 'I'll keep the room tidy though. You don't need to worry about a mess — I'm a very methodical worker and there'll be no bits and pieces scattered about, I promise you.'

She smiled. 'I won't worry about that. It will be your room and provided you don't make a lot of noise and you keep it clean it will be up to you. I wouldn't presume to dictate about anything else.'

'Then I can have it?' He sounded a little breathless.

'Yes. Let's say a month's trial.'

He was embarrassingly grateful. 'It's not easy to find somewhere in a seaside town except in the winter and it will be nice to have a place that's my own. Somewhere that I can put down roots as it were. I don't need much, you see. Just a private place.'

You and me both, she thought as she set about cooking a meal. Each in our own way, we need to put down roots. She hardly thought that that was what he was doing, but for her and Tim it was the beginning of that process. They had planted their roots now and they were spreading out like the branches of a sturdy tree.

However, Tim did not feel the same way as she did about their lodger.

'A lodger. Whatever for? I thought you didn't like people marching up and down stairs in that other place. You were always moaning about it. Now you want someone in here.'

'This is quite different.' Her voice was low, seductive. 'This will give us a steady income all year round. After all we only need one bedroom, and if we save his rent and live on your money, and mine when I can find another job for the evenings . . .'

'If that's what you want, Katie. Frankly I can't see the need for it. You've got your

47

house now, a place of your own just as you said. So why immediately start filling it with other people?'

'It will help pay the mortgage, darling, and be a safeguard should either of us lose our jobs. He'll be no trouble. He's a radio repair man, a quiet chap, and it would be silly not to use all the rooms after all. It's such a lovely house, Tim, and it's ours — or it will be one day. Doesn't that thrill you?'

Tim shrugged his shoulders and grinned at her. 'Not particularly. As long as we've a roof over our heads I'm not too bothered if it's ours or someone else's.' He gazed around the room. 'You've made it look nice, though. You're a born homemaker, Katie.' He moved closer and took her, rather clumsily, into his arms. 'I do love you so much, you know.'

6

Jonathan was a contented baby and Maureen was so happy with him. Sometimes, when he was asleep after his feed during the day she sat by the cot and simply looked at him. After all the years of frustration they had a baby, and such a beautiful baby. It was fate, she decided. Jonathan was meant for them and that was why they had had to wait so long. No other baby would have been right.

Gordon loved him too, although he wasn't as demonstrative with the child as she was. But when he was bigger, she thought, that's when men liked children best. Not when they were so small and perfect.

Occasionally she thought it wouldn't last, that no one could stay as happy as she was, but she always dismissed such thoughts quickly. She had had her problems and now she was one of the lucky ones. She had a baby, a husband, a fine house, friends . . . and maybe later, when Jonathan was older, they could have another child in the same way, a brother or sister for him.

For the baby's first Christmas Maureen decorated every nook and cranny in the house. She bought an enormous tree and some fairy lights. She delighted in looking round the shops and choosing presents for their son. Gordon pointed out that the baby was only three months old and couldn't care less whether it was Christmas or Easter. He was feeling rather left out. Expecting Maureen to be tied up with the new baby for the first few weeks he thought she should have settled Jonathan into a routine and be back to being a proper wife and helpmate to him again by now.

The first real crisis came on Christmas Eve when Maureen produced a Father Christmas outfit and wanted him to wear it to fill Jonathan's stocking. It had been a hectic morning in the office, then they'd had the staff party and by the time he got out on the road for the homeward journey the traffic was horrendous. It took nearly twice as long as usual. All he wanted was to get home and relax with a drink after his dinner.

'You've got to be joking,' he said. 'He's far too young to know what it's all about.'

'That has nothing to do with it. It's Christmas time and we have a child. Surely it's not too much trouble to do the traditional thing?'

He walked slowly over to the sideboard and poured himself a drink. 'Yes, it is. I'll do it when he's older, but I'm not playing charades for a three month old baby. You're obsessed with motherhood, Maureen, and it's not good for either you or Jonathan. Nor for me. I think that most of the time these days you forget you have a husband.'

She threw the outfit onto the chair and rushed upstairs. Gordon sighed but made no attempt to follow her. He knew exactly what she'd be doing: drooling over the baby, asleep in his cot. He was feeling totally neglected, while every sniffle, every nuance of the baby's expression was noted, recorded, photographed and followed up. Maureen gave up everything once she had her child. When he had suggested an evening out, a meal at a hotel where there was a dance floor, Maureen, who loved dancing even more than he did, wouldn't leave the baby with anyone. Her best friend and her husband, both of whom she had known since her schooldays had offered to come for the weekend but she still wouldn't go.

They made up their quarrel later that evening. Maureen even laughed faintly and admitted that it was a bit silly really, 'But I couldn't resist it when I saw the Santa outfit. Next year perhaps. He'll appreciate it then.'

Gordon doubted it but said nothing. On

Christmas morning he gave her a small, beautifully gift-wrapped box. Inside was a gold locket.

★ ★ ★

When Gordon said to her one evening that his firm were transferring their head office from London to Brighton and he thought they should consider moving, she pulled a face.

'The firm will pay the cost of a move. I shall be in a higher salary bracket but I will have an even greater work load,' he said. 'I'd like to cut down the travelling hours if I could and spend more time at home with you and young Johnnie. We could go down at the weekend and look at houses, what do you think?'

'It will upset Jonathan's routine.'

'Nonsense. He's a very adaptable baby.' Glancing down at the cot he smiled at the sleeping child. 'And as he grows he'll love living by the sea. I always wanted to when I was a boy and I'm looking forward to it now. Come on, Maureen,' he added coaxingly, 'having a baby in the house doesn't mean you can't ever do other things.'

They did go to Sussex at the weekend and they looked at several houses, but neither of them saw what they were really looking for. That was until late afternoon shortly before they were planning to return home.

'There's this one in Longsands,' the estate agent told them. 'Nice house, lovely garden, only a few years old.'

'Longsands. How far is that?'

'Under ten miles from Brighton. Pleasant town on the coast. It grew from a fishing village in the 1850s to a tourist town largely through the advent of the railways. In the 1950s' rebuilding programme after the last war Longsands not only replaced those buildings which were bombed, but attracted large numbers of business men and women with factories and shops in the surrounding area. It's a thriving place which derives its main revenue now from holiday-makers instead of fishing.' He looked across to Maureen, 'I think you'd like the house.'

In spite of Maureen's protestations that they had seen enough for that day Gordon insisted on going to look. Jonathan had gone to sleep and they followed the estate agent's car along the coast road to Longsands. They had opted to travel in their own car so they could start for home after viewing the property, without returning to Brighton.

It was warm for the time of year and the sea looked calm. There were even a few people strolling along the promenade. Boarding houses and hotels gleamed white in the wintry sunshine. At the end of the esplanade they turned sharply and climbed a steepish hill. At the top they were in a road where tantalizing glimpses of the shore caught them through the trees. Maureen relaxed. They turned off this cliff road and into the drive of a house on the corner.

The house was everything the details Maureen was looking at said it was: detached, spacious, walled garden at the back, double garage, luxury kitchen. 'I thought that was estate agent jargon,' Gordon said, 'but this one really does live up to it. I've never seen such splendour in a kitchen before, have you Maureen? Think you could work in it?'

Maureen was rapidly falling in love with the house. She had enjoyed the drive along the front too. It would be good to bring Jonathan up in such a healthy environment close to the sea.

'That long building we saw on the seafront,' she asked the agent, 'what is that?'

'That's a holiday camp, Mrs Linnet; but a small and very sedate one. It's owned by a private firm, not a big company. Also it's a long way from here. You can't even see it from this area because it's the other side of the curve of the bay.'

The back garden was extensive. A patio led to beautifully laid out flowerbeds and a lawn near the house. Beyond this were a trellis work archway and a screening hedge which hid a kitchen garden. Behind that was a delightful area of wild flowers. A revolving summerhouse on a smaller lawn to the side of the property completed the picture.

'You have the downs behind you and they can't be built on. There is a school within a quarter of an hour's drive, and in the town itself there are many individual shops as well as the larger ones. The resort of Brighton with its vast amenities is close enough to be convenient but far enough away for Longsands not to be affected by its day-trippers.'

They wandered through the house again on their own looking for snags and not finding any major ones. Driving home in the sudden coolness the evening brought with it Gordon said, 'What do you think?'

'Yes. If we have to move that's the only one I liked. What about you?'

'I'm for it, Maureen.'

They returned home, put their house on the market and negotiated for the Longsands one.

They were fortunate in having two interested buyers for their Surrey house and it sold quickly without them having to drop the price. They moved to Longsands towards the end of March when Jonathan was six months old, and all through the summer Maureen took her son along the front, onto the beach and introduced him to the sea. He loved the water as she held him above the little shore wavelets and jumped him up and down to get him used to it. He squealed with delight after the first shock of it hitting his feet and cried when she took him away and onto the large towel she had spread across the sand further up. Then into his pram with a bottle and either a walk back up the cliff road, or, if she had brought her car, a foray into the town to the library or the shops before returning home.

Longsands did not have a pleasure pier, but at the eastern end near the holiday camp there was a long jetty. The fishing boats launched from that end of the town too, and often sold some of the catch to people who had watched them coming in.

Once or twice Maureen walked eastwards towards the holiday camp. It seemed quiet enough — any noise was contained within its high walls. From the seafront you could not even see the chalets. Mainly though, she walked in the opposite direction, and as he grew she took her young son onto the sand at the west end of the town. It was always less crowded as, apart from being a long way from the centre of things, it was a greater expanse of sand because it reached right back into the bottom of the cliff. There were no stalls selling ice cream and candyfloss this end either but it was fine for Jonathan because of all the little pools of water that collected where the sand dipped. Time enough to let him venture further when he was older, she thought. At the moment she was his world even as he was hers.

She invited the neighbours in for drinks, joined in the local coffee mornings, taking Jonathan with her, usually asleep in his buggy. The one thing she wouldn't do was leave him with a babysitter and go out for the evening with Gordon. She was selfishly happy and totally engrossed with the baby. The little niggle that her son had superseded her husband in her affections was so small that most of the time she didn't notice it — just occasionally, when she caught Gordon looking at her rather sadly.

He drove his car into Brighton to work each day and relished not having to do the journey from London which he had done for so long. He was home hours earlier and also found time to pursue some of his hobbies. He joined a few clubs, some weekly and some monthly and suggested that Maureen do the same some evenings while he looked after their child; but she insisted that she was fine and had no need for any outside interests.

'What you mean is that you don't trust me with young Johnnie, isn't it?'

'If that's what you like to think, Gordon, but it isn't true. I simply love being with him — I want to enjoy his babyhood while I can. It is no hardship for me to stay with him. I waited so long and I don't want to start gallivanting about until he's much, much older.'

As Jonathan grew, taking his first steps and saying his first recognizable words, so Gordon became more and more enchanted by this tiny human being in his image. For his son was so very much like him, everyone they knew commented on it. Maureen might dote on the child in her way, but Gordon was his willing slave too.

As September edged August into the horizon and Jonathan's first birthday came into view they resolved their differences to give him a wonderful birthday party. That night, for the first time since the baby's arrival, Gordon drew Maureen into his arms and she responded.

By Christmas, however, they were back to being almost strangers. All her time, all her energy and all her thoughts were of and for Jonathan and there seemed no place left for Gordon. He loved his son, and gradually this love for the boy eased some of the ache in his heart.

7

The first time she had the dream, Katie woke with sweat almost pouring from her. She had been nursing a baby, a wrinkled little old man of a baby, and she had suddenly realized that he wasn't hers. She woke at that point and the relief when she did so was wonderful. Now she had this dream about once a week — sometimes she would go nine or ten days and then it would return. Always she woke at the point when she realized he wasn't hers.

In the cold light of dawn she began to think about the baby she had carried and birthed and wonder how he was faring. Ridiculous, she told herself, because I knew from the beginning that he would never be mine, nor did I want him to be.

She busied herself with the house, with cooking and dressmaking and with her job in the newsagent's in the town and an occasional stint as a waitress when extras were needed for a special function at one of the hotels. Sometimes, at weekends she stayed and drank a cup of tea with John when she went to his room to collect the rent. He kept the place tidy as he had promised to do, although she truly wasn't bothered about that anyway. She knew nothing about the insides of radios yet his enthusiasm for his work and hobby overflowed when he talked about it, and, in spite of herself she was interested.

Tim had little to do with him. 'As long as you're happy with the arrangement then it's okay by me,' he told her, 'and I suppose you're right in the fact that we don't need that extra room, so it may as well earn its keep.'

Since their move Tim had been consistently in work and it looked as though the bar where he was now employed in the evenings would be keeping him on for the winter. He still worked at the camp during the daytime, helping with the painting and general maintenance. 'Some of the larger camps are taking autumn and winter bookings, doing special weekends and three and four day holidays,' he told her after one of the management and staff meetings. 'Our lot decided not to go down that road at present anyway. You need to be able to attract the big stars for the entertainment out of season, and we aren't in the league for doing that. Ours is very much for family holidays still.'

★   ★   ★

One evening just before Christmas Katie began to work out their finances in greater detail. When Tim came in she placed a mug of tea and a large chunk of homemade fruit cake in front of him and said, 'Tim, I've been thinking that we could possibly move from here sometime next year.'

'Move! Whatever for? We've only been here a few months. Don't you like the place anymore?'

'Of course I do, but it's a stepping stone. You knew that when we bought it. I've been watching house prices and already we could make a profit on this place and go for something better.'

He had a piece of cake halfway to his mouth and he carefully replaced it on the plate. Then he stood up and came towards her.

'Katie, I go along with most of the things you want but I'm not prepared to keep uprooting, you know. This place is nice. It's cosy. I agree with you that it's a vast improvement on the flat; I hadn't realized how uncomfortable that was until we moved here, but this is great. I don't want the upheaval of moving every time we get settled in somewhere.'

'It's the way to get on. Buying and selling. All we needed was the start. I always knew — '

'That's as maybe, but . . . '

'You won't need to do anything, Tim. I'll see to it all. I enjoy doing it. All you'll need to see to is the signature. And it won't be yet. A year, eighteen months, something like that. But when I find a place I like I'll tell you and we can go and look together. There's no harm in doing that now, is there?'

'I see nothing wrong with — '

'Of course there isn't. It's a lovely house — our first, our very own. Or it will be when the mortgage is paid off, which will happen much faster with a bit of buying and selling.'

'What about our lodger.'

'John can come with us if he wants to. The sort of place I have in mind will have enough bedrooms for two lodgers, or maybe even three . . . ' She wound her arms round his neck. 'Finish your supper and come to bed. I shan't even start looking until after Christmas, so there's no need for you to worry. I just wanted us to think about it so we could make our plans.'

It was a start, she thought later. Gradually all the things she wanted and hoped for would happen. Hadn't she proved that already? Once Tim was used to the idea he wouldn't make a fuss. He would be happy and comfortable, he had said as much about this place tonight. He simply didn't care for the preplanning but once it was a fact he was content. In any case she would do all the business of the new house. All he would need to do would be to look over it with her, to keep himself in the picture. And of course, to sign the necessary documents. If he didn't like the property too then they wouldn't go ahead and she would look for something else.

There was another reason Katie concentrated her thoughts on a move: the dream. She had it regularly once a week now, sometimes twice, and it worried her. Was the baby all right? She didn't even know his name or where he lived. No reason why she should, she told herself sternly. It had worked. Two people who wanted a child now had one and she and Tim were getting on their feet. Why, they could even afford to take a holiday if they wanted, and maybe this winter when things slackened off at the camp they would. Do them both good. Might even put a bit of romance back into their lives. But she hoped the baby was all right. She had carried him for nine months, and, in spite of her intentions, she couldn't help worrying over him a bit when he kept recurring in her dreams.

She mentioned a likely move to John a few months later before they asked the agent round to assess the house. 'We shall definitely be staying in the town so if you would like to move with us that will be fine.'

John looked at her in surprise. 'Well, that's nice of you, Mrs Bray. Obviously I'd need to leave here because you would want to sell with vacant possession. I can see that. Yes, I'd like to move with you if there's room for me and my bits and pieces.' He glanced at the radio paraphernalia which was spread across the large table in the corner of the room.

'Oh, yes. It will probably be a slightly larger house, I may even take guests in the summer but your room will be there for you all year round, John.'

The house agent came round one evening, clipboard in hand. He went through the house, measuring and writing and even tapping the walls in one of the rooms.

John was washing up in his curtained off kitchen area and the estate agent said curtly. 'You are selling with vacant possession, aren't you?'

'Yes, of course. Jo — Mr Jones is moving with us.'

Tim was barely polite. She had thought that he was used to the idea and she was embarrassed by his monosyllabic answers. The estate agent addressed all his questions and remarks to Tim of course. Her anger seethed as she went with the agent to the front door when he was leaving. Tim was sitting in the armchair looking at the paper when she returned. It was his night off from the holiday camp and she had wanted them both to be there. Now she wished she had asked the man to come when he was at work.

'I hope you aren't going to behave like that with prospective buyers,' she snapped.

'Look, Katie, I'm perfectly happy here. Okay, if you want to sell and make some money, that's fine, but don't expect me to fall over myself about it.'

'That'd be the day.' She tossed her head and went through to the kitchen, glad that he would be at work when the photographer came tomorrow afternoon. She had made sure that it would be on her half-day from the shop. She might even ask him to take a photograph of the interior, perhaps showing the good oak occasional table Mr Pugh had found for her only the other week. That would make it look like a really classy residence.

The house sold quickly. Although they dropped £500 on the deal she knew it was better to do that because she had already seen what she wanted. The property was a good distance from the sea, but being at the top of a hill there was a glimpse from the attic bedroom window. Buses ran past the door but the most important aspect for Katie was the size of the house; it had four good bedrooms, a lounge, dining room, kitchen, bathroom and two lavatories. There were other guest houses in the road and it seemed obvious to her that visitors to the town didn't mind being ten minutes from the seafront.

'After all,' she said to John when he came in from work one evening and drank a cup of tea with her while she was preparing a meal in her kitchen, 'they are on holiday and time is no object. Besides, it's cheaper up there. They charge the earth on the seafront. Even those small hotels in the little side roads just off the promenade are very expensive.'

Tim went with her to look at the place she had chosen. 'It's a good way from my work,' he said.

'Oh, Tim. There's frequent buses, and you could walk there in ten minutes if you cut down the Dupont Steps.' The steps led to the town and the shops, and from there you were only minutes away from the promenade. 'You'd pay three or four times what we're paying to get a house like this nearer the seafront.'

'I can't see the need to move anyway,' he grumbled, 'and look at the state of the place. It's falling to pieces, that's why it's cheap.'

'No it isn't. The building society wouldn't lend us money on it if that were true. All it needs is a coat of paint and some emulsion and it will look lovely. Just as good as the rest of them along here, you'll see. And when it's done we'll earn money in the summer and maybe go on holiday during the off season. That would tie in very well with your job at the camp and we really will be moving up the ladder.'

'It's important for you to do that, isn't it, Katie?'

'What, move up? Yes, it is. But you knew that when we married. Agreed to it even. I can hear you now, 'Whatever you want, Katie', you said, 'you know I'll go along with anything'. Well, this is what I want now Tim. You should be glad I'm ambitious. Already we're both enjoying a better kind of life than either of our parents had.'

'My mum was happy enough. She had her cat and dog, her little garden, the sea down the road. She never yearned for something bigger just for the sake of it.'

She didn't flare at him this time. Instead she was very quiet. 'I don't think this conversation is getting us anywhere. If you really don't like it I'll tell the agent no and look for something else. But be sure, Tim, because if we let this go the next one may not be such a bargain.'

She followed his silence out of the house.

8

'Hey daydreamer, where's your usual happy smile,' one of the waitresses called to Tim the next day as he went about his work.

He looked up as she came towards him, her long, honey-coloured hair falling softly about her shoulders. Usually she had her hair up and Tim thought how lovely it looked now framing her attractive face.

'You have pretty hair,' he said, feeling as surprised as she looked when the words came out.

She gave a mock curtsy, 'Thank you, kind sir.'

Embarrassed, he turned away but she caught his hand. 'Tim. I was only teasing. I'm glad you think I'm pretty. As a matter of fact I think you're great. Handsome . . . ' He eased his hand from hers and she fell into step beside him as other people appeared.

'As I was saying, handsome and clever in a quiet way and I bet you're a great lover.'

'Listen, I'm married, Betty.'

'So are half the guys I go out with. You can kiss me if you like. No strings.'

They both saw the manager approaching at

that moment. Tim heard her mutter, 'damn', and took the opportunity to pretend that was who he was looking for. Betty moved on, both dazzling and confusing him for a moment with her smile. He managed to avoid her until the evening, when they were both in the tiny passage leading to the kitchen for a few moments with no one else around.

'Tim,' Her voice was soft, seductive. 'I meant it. Nobody need know.'

'Betty, you — you're a very nice girl, an attractive person, and — and if I was single, I'd jump at the chance, but . . .'

Two bright spots burned on her cheeks and she flounced round. Her hair was now sedately settled in a huge twist on top of her head, and, with a quick movement she adjusted the inadequate sort of frill all the waitresses wore when they were on duty.

'Bit of a goody-goody, are you? How unexciting. But this morning you nearly broke out of your shell, didn't you, Mr Nice Guy? Well, it's your loss, not mine. There's plenty of fellows who will.' Then she was gone.

Tim stood there, feeling a fool. She wasn't the first girl to give him the eye since he had worked at the camp, but she was the most blatant, and it didn't help his ego a jot to know that he had asked for it. Whatever had made him comment on her hair this morning?

'Hi, Tim. Come on, don't stand there dreaming.' Suddenly the lull was over and the passage became a seething mass of humanity with waiters and waitresses rushing about, talk and laughter filling the air. He pushed open the door leading into the kitchen and set about his evening's work. He saw Betty dashing around and heard her too because she wasn't the quietest girl on the camp. It amazed him that she should think of him in a sexual context. She was pretty, he thought, but not his type. It was years since he had thought of any girl except Katie like that. Well, maybe not — he'd noticed if someone had nice legs or a wolf-whistle figure but it never stirred him beyond the noticing.

Walking home very late that night he thought about Katie. There never had been anyone in his heart but her. From the moment they met she had filled his life. He knew she was so much more ambitious than he was, and, in a strange sort of way this too appealed to him. She was so alive, so vibrant about everything and he had admired this part of her nature. Since their marriage this very quality that had once stimulated him often annoyed him, but it was part of her personality. The attraction of opposites, he thought. Sometimes I wish I too could be like that; powerful, a leader.

The business tonight with Betty had startled him. Smiling to himself now, he wondered what Katie would say. Not that he was going to tell her, of course. No point in starting a scene and he knew she would create one if he mentioned it even in a light-hearted sort of way.

He hadn't thought about that before. How would she handle it if it happened to her? Would she be tempted? At home he quietly climbed into bed beside her. A great fear gripped him and he reached out and laid his hand on her breast. She stirred, slowly at first, then, turning towards him she murmured, 'My baby, oh my baby.' At least that's what it sounded like.

★　★　★

Katie worked hard in her boarding house. They moved at the end of February and for the next month the place seemed littered with ladders and workmen.

'Sometimes I can't understand you, Katie,' Tim said one evening as they ate their meal. It was that rare day that came about every couple of months when he had a complete day off. 'One of the things you disliked most about that first flat was people in and out, up and down the stairs every day. Yet ever since we've moved you have deliberately filled the house with people. First, John, and now you're planning on having hordes of holiday-makers. It doesn't make sense, darling.'

'But it's a wonderful way to make money and to eventually have the place of our dreams. A couple of years here and — '

'Of your dreams, Katie. The place of your dreams. I was satisfied with the first house. I agree it was a vast improvement on the flat — you were absolutely right about that — but this restlessness now . . . '

She smiled at his words. 'Leave it to me, Tim darling. I love juggling about with this sort of thing. I didn't know that I would, not that first time of course, but it's so easy once you've started.'

'Meaning that as soon as we're settled here and are nice and cosy you'll want to up sticks and move again?'

His tone this time was more teasingly affectionate than angry, and she felt glad. The one flaw that was spoiling her enjoyment in her new-found hobby was her husband's attitude and she didn't want to push him beyond the limits of his patience. His contentment with his lot, and her ambition for improvement were growing at the same rate, and they were widening the gap that had appeared between them.

Tim never mentioned the money that had enabled them to buy the first property. Unless he did Katie knew she could never again talk to him about it. Nor could she talk to anyone else and the nightmares continued. She had thought that they might stop when she was no longer living in the house bought with the money earned from her surrogacy, but they were as frequent as ever. At least once every week she woke drenched in sweat and hugging a newborn infant to her breast. Often it was two or three times. She never thought about the baby when she was busy but at night she was powerless to stop what was happening to her.

Tim was busy at the camp, but he did help a little with the decorating of the new house. Mostly though, it was Katie who had a paintbrush in her hand. John volunteered to decorate his room and the small army of workmen concentrated on the visitors' rooms and the outside of the property. When it was finished she took several photographs from various angles and advertised in papers and brochures. 'Vacancies throughout the season. Good food, comfortable surroundings, under new management.'

She also gave her notice in at the

newsagent's, telling them of her plans for the guest house. She had got on well with the owner and his wife and they wished her well and gave her a good pen and pencil set the day she left. 'For you to write your future bookings with,' it said on the accompanying good luck card.

All the rooms were spacious and John was delighted with his. Katie turned the lounge into a bedroom for herself and Tim, bought a kneehole desk from George Pugh at the antiques shop and set about the business of becoming a guest house owner.

Tim protested mildly about using the lounge as a bedroom.

'It gives us three to let, darling,' she said softly, winding her arms round his neck. 'While I'm cleaning and cooking for four or five people it's not much extra to do so for six or seven now, is it? And that room is so big. There's masses of space to use the far end as our own private lounge. With the television and settee down there . . . '

He shrugged. 'I suppose so. In any case I see enough of holidaymakers at the camp without coming home to them as well. So maybe it'll work if it effectively separates them from us.'

The guest house did well. There were some empty weeks and as they were not on the main route through the town they never filled in with touring casuals looking for a place overnight; but her earnings justified the hard work. She did bed and breakfast and also bed, breakfast and evening meals.

In July Katie employed a young girl to help in the house. In spite of being very tired when she went to her bed at night, she still experienced the dream about the baby frequently. Once or twice she cried out in her anguish and Tim held her tightly and murmured softly to her. This added a new fear — that she might talk about the baby in these dreams. How would Tim react to that? The idea had been abhorrent to him from the start and if he saw that it was now having an effect on her . . .

Angrily she chided herself. It wasn't what she did that was bothering her. She had gone into it with her eyes open and it had been the salvation of their marriage. If they had still been in that grotty little flat, arguing daily, existing rather than living, their marriage would have broken down. Of that she was convinced.

She wished she could tell Tim about her fears. Why should she dream about the child now if he was thriving? Or perhaps it was nothing to do with the state of the baby, but something within herself.

When she went shopping one day she realized, quite suddenly, what the trouble was: she was noticing the babies. Why, she even bent over prams to talk to them, and that had never been her style. Was this, perhaps, the cause of the recurring dream? Was she secretly longing for a child? Why not? she asked herself in the privacy of her bath. She placed her hands across her stomach and remembered the time she had been carrying the other child. What if she and Tim had one of their own?

She broached the subject to him that night. 'We could afford a child now, Tim, and we love each other — '

'There you go again, money. It's always money, isn't it, Katie? You never used to be like this.'

'Yes, I did,' she flared, 'only you were too comatose to notice. I've never hankered after being a millionaire, but I have always wanted some of the good things, the things money can buy. We have some of them now and we could give a child a decent life, a comfortable environment, a good education. Don't you want a son or daughter, Tim? We'd be a real family then.'

'Katie, if it's what you want then the answer is yes. I guess it'd be okay having a kid about the place. You've not wanted one before, or so you said . . . '

'But now — '

'I know,' he said, anticipating her words, but this time with a grin on his face, 'we couldn't afford it then but now we can.'

By the end of the year, when Katie still wasn't pregnant she became very distressed. The last visitors of the season had gone home, she had cleaned and polished, and even moved herself and Tim into one of the upstairs bedrooms while they redecorated theirs. She tried to believe that it didn't matter, that it wasn't meant to be. She could carry a child for someone else but it wasn't destined that she could conceive one of her own.

Without telling Tim she visited the doctor and haltingly told him of her desire to be a mother.

'How long have you been married?' he asked.

'Seven years.'

'How long have you been trying for a family?'

'Almost a year, doctor.'

'And you did once have a child,' he said gently, after he had examined her.

She hadn't expected that.

'Yes. Yes, I did.' Thinking quickly she said, 'It — it was adopted. It happened a long while ago.'

'Perhaps I had better see your husband. Don't worry,' he added when he saw her panic-stricken expression, 'I will not say anything about a previous pregnancy. You are not the first woman in this situation, you know.'

Lowering her gaze from his face, as she realized the implication he had put on his knowledge, she listened to the soothing voice saying, 'I suggest that when I ask your husband to undergo tests, you are prepared to do the same. We know you can conceive and carry a child but it will, in this instance be better for you both to be tested, I believe.'

She thought that she would have a difficult job to persuade Tim to visit the doctor, but it proved surprisingly easy.

'Okay, Katie, if you want a child so much, we'll both go for tests,' he said. 'But I can already tell you why you haven't conceived.'

Trembling now she sat on the edge of the bed.

'You — you can?'

'Of course. It's very simple. You are being too intense about the whole thing. It's a well known fact. If you relax everything will be fine, you'll see.' Hovering between laughter and tears Katie threw her arms round her husband. 'You could be right,' she said, remembering her dreams.

The tests were carried out at the local hospital. Katie, sure in her mind now that Tim was right about her not being relaxed enough to conceive was shocked when the results came through. Tim was mentally paralysed.

'It's ridiculous,' he shouted. 'Me not being able to father a child. Utter nonsense, that bloody doctor doesn't know what he's talking about.' The tirade went on and on as he stood, pale-faced and stiff. The only movement was the rapid clenching and unclenching of his hands. She did not know how to handle the situation.

'We could adopt a baby,' she said eventually.

'Adopt. Adopt. Oh, no. Let someone else have a baby for us, after you once had one for someone else.' He was striding up and down the room now.

'Keep your voice down a bit, Tim. John's upstairs. He'll hear you.'

'Let him. Let the whole bloody world know.'

Never before had she seen this side of her husband. Gentle, easy-going Tim, who always took the line of least resistance, who seldom raised his voice or swore.

'Those tests aren't conclusive, you know. Even doctors can sometimes be wrong. We could . . . '

'We're having no more tests. We should never have submitted to that one. You've got your big house now, you can't have a child too, so you may as well get used to the idea quickly. Now I want to hear no more on the subject.'

She felt desperately sorry for him and tried to put her arm about him but he roughly pushed it away. 'Leave it, Katie. It's not the end of the world. I'm going to work and you had better find something else to do too now the season is over.'

He took his coat from the hook and left, slamming the door behind him.

9

John usually ate in a small café in the town at lunchtimes, but he returned home because he had changed his trousers that morning and forgotten to transfer his money to the clean pair. He heard the muffled sobbing as he walked through the hall. He knew Tim was at work and hesitated, but after a few moments he went upstairs. After putting his wallet and loose change into his trouser pockets he was back, standing outside the door. Should he see what was wrong? Mrs Bray had looked very poorly lately and he suspected that all was not well between her and her husband. He had heard raised voices a lot in the weeks since the summer visitors had left.

John didn't want to interfere, yet he could hardly ignore the sounds which had grown louder. It might be nothing to do with the marriage. She could have fallen and hurt herself. He tapped on the door. When there was no reply he knocked again, and the crying caught on a sob and stopped.

'W-who is it?'

'It's me — John. Are you all right, Mrs Bray?'

'Just a minute.'

He stood there awkwardly until she opened the door. Her eyes were red-rimmed but she had obviously washed her face and brushed her hair.

'John, I — I wasn't expecting you back yet,' she said. 'What — what did you want?'

'Nothing really, Mrs Bray. I — well, I thought I heard a noise and, knowing you were alone . . . '

Suddenly her face seemed to crumple. 'Oh, John, you're a very sweet boy,' she said. 'You heard me crying, didn't you? I'm sorry about that. It's nothing really. Just feeling a bit down you know. Look, come in. Got time for a cup of tea?'

She didn't try to explain her tears beyond saying, 'Tim and I had a little tiff this morning, John, and I guess it upset me more than I realized at the time. It was silly, but I'm okay now. Don't tell him, will you?'

'No, of course not.'

'Guess I haven't enough to do now the visitors have left.' Her voice was still a little unsteady. 'Now you would immerse yourself in your radio hobby, wouldn't you? But I haven't an interest like that to occupy me.'

'There's lots of clubs in the town,' he said eagerly, as he followed her into the kitchen to make the tea. 'Photography, painting, writing, dressmaking — '

'Hey, wait a minute. I'm not exactly looking for work.'

He laughed and so did she.

'Thanks. And sorry I made such a fool of myself. Maybe it's not such a bad idea to join something for the winter now the decorating's finished. Where would I find out about these clubs?'

'In the library, Mrs Bray. There's a list of them all and of when and where they meet.'

Tim was in a better mood when he returned from work later that night.

'Wages are going up when the season starts,' he said. 'What sort of a day have you had?'

'Fine.'

'Katie?'

'Yes, Tim.'

'Come to bed,' he said.

Maybe things were settling down after all, she thought. Maybe one day they would return to the old camaraderie and loving they'd had when they first fell in love. Those were the days when Tim had promised her the moon and stars. 'I love you so much, Katie, I'd give you anything you wanted.' Well in a way he had, she thought. She had forged ahead without too much opposition once she had made her mind up about something. If only she could undo the last few months she would.

'Come on, Katie. What are you doing?'

Climbing into bed she snuggled into her husband's arms.

* ★ *

Katie went into the library a few days later, and studied the lists of activities offered. The two that appealed to her the most were a painting group and a writers' circle. She had no experience of either, but she had often had a yearning to be an artist or a novelist. Maybe now was the time to find out if she had any talents in those directions. At least it would keep her mind from babies.

She settled for the writers' circle because it met once a week, while the painting group was once a month. She wanted her therapy more frequently than that.

They met in a room over a pub. It was warm and friendly and when she walked in someone immediately spoke to her. She felt awful when she admitted that she had not actually written anything yet, but they didn't seem to mind and took it for granted that she wanted to write, otherwise why would she be there?

She listened intently that first evening, both

to the stories and articles read out, and to the comments about them from the other members. When asked to give her opinion she found it fairly easy to do so, and to admit that, although a great reader, she had never actually attempted to write a story as yet. There was a good atmosphere, and she returned home filled with ideas. The following day she went into town and bought herself half a dozen soft pencils and a fat notebook.

There were usually between twelve and fifteen people at the meetings. Katie soon became familiar with their names and their writing. She took a short piece along herself that second time. It was an article about running a guest house and it was well received. Most of the members thought it should be longer and use more humorous incidents. She had begun it with a funny situation and several of them said they thought she had a good touch for this kind of writing.

'It's not easy to make people laugh,' Gordon, a short story writer said to her afterwards. 'Do try something else along those lines.'

She still experienced the dream of the baby, and he was always a baby in it, although the child she had carried for nine months would now be three years old. Perhaps she should try to write it out of her system, she thought. Not what really happened, but a story about a girl who gave her baby up for another reason. Except, of course, this particular baby never was hers.

She and Tim were often edgy with each other again and she tried not to think about the old days, nor yet how much she loved him. She knew she was much stronger than Tim. Perhaps most women were stronger than most men, she reflected, but he had taken a bitter blow to his manhood, and, although she felt he was mistakenly blaming her for this, she could understand his moods most of the time.

Since joining the writers' circle she analysed herself more than previously, and she knew she needed something to do. The guest house partially satisfied this need during the summer; now she had her writing activities too. Even if she never had anything published at all she still got a buzz from doing it. If only Tim were happier she could possibly be content.

Their marriage had deteriorated. They were sometimes like two people living in the same house as friends, or even as lodgers, as John was . . . She often wept for the loving closeness they had once enjoyed and cursed her sweeping ambitions of going up in the world for its loss. When they were in that grotty flat she needed to push them up and out of it. It had been a challenge and perhaps she was destined to always need such an incentive.

Surely Tim knew how much she loved him — but these days he never let her near enough to his heart for her to tell him again. Sometimes it seemed that they had recaptured the old ecstasy for a while, yet in the mornings all was cool and distant again, the passion of the night spent.

They had a blazing row just before she left for the writers' circle one evening. Tim, who should have been working late, arrived home as she was changing.

'You're not going out this evening, are you?' he said.

'Yes. It's circle night. I didn't expect you yet. I've left some food in the oven. It only needs warming through. I thought I would be back by the time you came in.'

'I changed shifts with Dave. He's got something important on tonight.'

'Here, I'll switch the oven on for you,' she said, disappearing into the kitchen. 'Keep your eye on it though, or it'll burn.'

'You're still going out then?'

Looking at him in surprise she said, 'Yes, of

course I am. I enjoy it, and I didn't know you'd be home early. Another few minutes and I would have been gone anyway.'

'Got a boyfriend there I suppose. You've looked a lot happier lately, I've noticed. What do you do? Read your diaries to each other?'

'Tim. That's an awful accusation to make. There are men in the circle, yes, but I'm not interested in them any more than they are in me. We all have a mutual hobby and I won't let you spoil it with your dirty mind.'

'Dirty mind, is it . . . ?'

Ten minutes later when she went through the front door Katie wondered how they had become embroiled in such an argument so quickly and so fiercely. Tossing back her long hair she walked swiftly along the road. She would be late, but not too much and she had no intention now of not going to the meeting. If Tim didn't like it he could do the other thing . . . Her cheeks flamed as she recalled some of his remarks.

At the meeting she willed herself to concentrate on what was being read and discussed and to cut out the angry words which had been twirling round and round in her head. Afterwards she went with several of the group for coffee. They had asked her before but she had always refused because she wanted to get back. But tonight she only wanted to make Tim suffer. Coming home and expecting her to fall in with his changed plans, and with never a thought for her evening. It was unlike Tim to start an argument, and even more out of character for him to say such hurtful things. He had always been the peacemaker, not the instigator, she thought.

In the café she sat between Gordon and a woman called Ann who wrote romances. 'Not had one published yet,' she said to them both, 'but even Barbara Cartland had to begin somewhere.'

When they left Gordon offered to run her home. 'My car is in the central car park. It won't take long and it's such a cold night.'

She and Tim were cool with each other for a couple of days, there was none of the quick making up that had characterized previous flare-ups. He also seemed to be taking up more work at the camp. I must be patient, she told herself, he had an enormous blow and it will take time for him to recover. The worst part was that, whereas once he would have turned to her for help, now he didn't. He simply refused to talk about the fact that he could not give her a child.

After that first time of dropping her off at her house Gordon always offered her a lift. She sometimes demurred but they usually ended up riding home together. She learnt that his wife, Maureen, wasn't interested in writing. 'Cookery is more her thing, but in any case we are both glad of evenings apart. We don't get on well any more.'

'That's sad,' she said, thinking of herself and Tim. 'But you still love her . . . '

'We stay together for our son's sake. Maybe when he's older we'll go our separate ways. How about you, Katie? I know very little.' Later she thought that he hadn't really answered her question. She hadn't told him much about herself either. She somehow felt that it would be disloyal to Tim. Like telling tales out of school.

In the spring she was busy preparing the guest house for the season. The bookings were good, coming in well. There were several recommendations from last year's guests, which pleased her enormously. She had come to terms with the dream of the baby. It occurred roughly once a month now and was so vivid that she always woke feeling totally bereaved, and often sobbing. Sometimes Tim's arms were around her, his face close to hers in comfort, yet they never discussed it.

She had filled three fat notebooks with her writings but hadn't found the courage as yet to write about the baby she longed for more than ever. Not that one, she told herself. He was never mine. Perhaps if I hadn't seen him, held him for those few moments, I wouldn't be feeling like this now. Who could tell? Maybe the yearning would be there anyway.

10

She met Gordon at the entrance to the pub. His usual welcoming smile seemed distant, only half there, and without thinking she said, 'You look like I feel tonight, Gordon.'

He turned towards her then, as if seeing her properly. 'Does it show that much, Katie? Sorry.'

'No need. I was being terribly intrusive.'

They were inside the pub now and he said, 'To tell the truth I was only in half a mind to come tonight. Felt more like a walk along the front to forget my problems; but I'm not a great one for my own company.'

'I'm not much in the mood for circle either,' she said. 'Let's do that. Let the sea blow our troubles away for an hour, Gordon.'

He brightened immediately. 'You sure?'

'Positive. Come on, before anyone realizes we're here.'

They hurried out, down the road and round the corner without meeting any other member. Slowing down Gordon laughed wryly. 'I feel like a criminal, don't you?'

'I suppose so. I do enjoy the meetings, but,

like you, I would rather be out in the air tonight.'

They reached the promenade and for a few moments sauntered along together without speaking. Then she said, 'Isn't it strange how people change, Gordon? Tim used to be so gentle, so caring. I was always the pushy one. He used to say I was too ambitious, but now . . . '

'I'm listening,' he said quietly.

'He hasn't changed in a big way. At least I don't think he has. I mean, he's still not ambitious or anything but he's altered in the smaller things, the nice things.'

'Something must have made him change, don't you think?'

'Yes, I — I suppose so. But that's life, isn't it? Nothing stays the same, it can't.'

His hand touched hers as they walked along. It was the merest brush yet it set her blood tingling in her veins. She slipped her hand away from his. 'Anyway, you don't want to hear about my troubles, you've got some of your own. I'll shut up.'

'No, Katie, it's all right and sometimes it helps to talk about them.' His hand touched and then held hers again, directing her gently towards the railings. Together they stood there, gazing out to sea. Then he moved his hand from hers with a murmured, 'Sorry.

Would you believe me if I told you that I've been wanting to hold your hand for some time now?'

When she didn't answer he turned to look into her eyes, 'Katie.'

'Yes, Gordon.'

'I think I'm falling in love with you. After each meeting I — '

'You mustn't, Gordon. Oh, you mustn't.'

'Why?' His voice was little more than a whisper, his eyes tenderly questioning.

'Because of Tim and — and your wife.'

'Maureen and I are washed up, Katie. There's nothing there any more, except the boy. We stay together for his sake but we don't do things together any more. We are polite to each other, like two strangers who are trying to make something work. Katie, can you guess how my heart is behaving at this moment? Can you — '

'Gordon, please listen. Tim and I had a row tonight but it doesn't mean I don't love him, or that we don't love each other. We do.' Fumbling in her bag she found her handkerchief.

'Forgive me. Look, let's go for a coffee. We'll even talk about something else if you like.'

They talked about writing but without much enthusiasm and as they walked back to the car park afterwards he put his hand beneath her elbow.

That night, listening to Tim snoring and snorting beside her, the remembrance of Gordon's hand touching hers as they had stood by the railings looking out to sea made her nerve ends tingle and shiver with pleasure. It would have been so easy to respond to him. He mustn't ever know how easy. He hadn't touched her again but she recalled his words as he opened the car door for her when they reached her home. 'You will be at the next meeting, won't you, Katie. Please?'

A few evenings later Tim came in from work and said, 'I've got to go on a course. If I refuse I shall probably lose the job. If I accept it may mean promotion.'

'Oh Tim, that's good.'

'It's a bit of a bind.'

Katie laughed. 'Darling, you're always so enthusiastic about things. If I didn't know you I'd say you really meant that.'

'I do, and there's no call to be so sarcastic. I'm happy enough plodding along as we are now, but suddenly the management think we need extra training so they uproot us and spend a lot of money for nothing.'

Katie was still grinning broadly and slowly a smile lit up his face too, giving her a glimpse of the old Tim. 'I suppose they know what they're doing, but I hate all these upheavals.'

Tim left on the Sunday. She walked to the railway station with him then went onto the seafront for a while before turning for home. It was a clear, calm day. She loved the sea when it was shimmering with gentle movement as it was today, and when it was raging with foam and spitting over the railings with temper. When it was like that she donned her mackintosh and boots and walked the length of the esplanade, usually returning invigorated and content. She thought that nature had a way of purging itself of its frustrations with wind and storms and there were times when she wished that humans had the power of this outlet too. Her own tempers and passions seemed miniscule compared to the grandness of a rough sea.

On Monday she went for a walk in the early evening and met John as he returned from work. The telephone was ringing as she opened the front door. It was Tim.

'Where were you, Katie? I've tried three times.'

'Out walking. Why? Is it something urgent, Tim?'

John slipped past her and started up the

stairs to his room, but he knocked against a copper vase she had placed on the tiny landing and it made a terrific noise as it tumbled down the stairs.

'What on earth was that, Katie?'

'Only a vase I bought earlier today. John knocked it over as he went upstairs. I should have warned him it was there, I suppose.'

'What's John doing down with you anyway, Katie?'

She made a superhuman effort to control the temper she felt rising inside her, but only partially succeeded.

'He wasn't 'down with me' as you put it. He has just come in from work and we met at the front door.' She couldn't resist adding, 'Satisfied?'

On Tuesday she went to the writers' circle meeting. Gordon came in just as the chairman had started. He took a chair from the stack against the wall and placed it next to her end one. Turning to smile at him she was worried by the angry expression on his face. Halfway through a story that was being read out he nudged his notebook across to her and she read, *Will you come for a coffee with me afterwards? No hanky-panky I promise. Please say yes.*

Praying that the rush of blood to her cheeks wasn't as obvious as it felt she wrote

YES in bold letters, then passed the book back to him.

They went into the café they had visited previously, found a table for two in the corner and sat opposite each other silently for a few moments.

'It's all right, Katie. I just want to look at you, to be with you. I know you don't feel the same but let me have this brief time with you. I shan't see you for a whole week. Tim has you there all the while.'

'It's a dangerous game we're playing, Gordon.'

'I'm not playing, my dear, my very dear. I know it isn't the same between you and Tim as it is between Maureen and me, but,' his voice dropped into an even lower, gruffer tone, 'it means so much to me to be with you, even briefly like this.'

She was surprised at tears in her eyes, and hastily blinked them away.

'Things aren't — right between us. Some of it's my ambition I think. Tim's a bit of a stick-in-the-mud really and I keep uprooting him and moving us on. You wouldn't believe the place we were living in only a few years ago, Gordon.'

'Tell me about it.'

Once started she couldn't seem to stop. Never before had she put into words her revulsion for that flat during their final two years there. 'I'd have done anything to get out, to have a place of our own, however tiny. Somewhere private. Our own particular haven.'

'And how did you manage it?'

The memory sent the blood coursing through her veins. 'I — worked — extra. Did — all sorts of jobs. Earned the money,' she said, hoping her voice wasn't sounding as odd as it felt, seemingly strangled up in her throat.

'Good for you. I haven't had that sort of problem. Maureen has always been as ambitious as me. Strange really, but I've not thought of it as ambition before, Katie. We were never as poor as you I suppose, but, although far from rich, really rich I mean, we've always managed. Always had enough to live well. We both worked for years, of course, until the advent of the baby.'

'What's he like, your little boy?'

Gordon reached into his jacket pocket and from his wallet he produced a photograph of a fair-haired, chubby toddler.

'He was one in that picture. He's a real little imp but we both adore him. I was speaking the truth, Katie, when I told you he's the reason we are still together . . . '

His eyes caressed her. 'You and Tim have no family?'

'No.' Keeping her voice very steady she said as she handed the photograph back to him, 'It just didn't happen. Maybe it's as well as we seem to quarrel so much these days. But it wasn't always like that, Gordon. When we first married we had so many dreams and plans. Tim is a very contented person you know. He accepts conditions easily, but I don't. Just the way we're made I suppose.'

'Has it helped to talk about it, Katie?'

She nodded, suddenly unable to speak for the tears running freely down her cheeks.

'Katie. Oh, my darling, please don't cry. Please, I can't bear to see you so unhappy.'

Swiftly he came round to her side of the table and wrapped his arms around her. She buried her head into the rough tweediness of his jacket.

When he took her home he said, 'Will you be all right? Tim won't query why you're so much later than usual?'

'Tim isn't here, Gordon. He's on a course all this week, for the holiday camp where he works.'

It seemed to Katie that they looked at each other for a long, long time, yet when she thought about it later she knew it had only been a moment. A moment of destiny.

'You could — come in for a coffee if you like, Gordon.'

11

Maureen wasn't sure when she knew that Gordon was involved with another woman. She never discovered a note or letter in his pocket, nor lipstick on his collar. There was not even a sudden, illuminating moment when he said something and she realized. Yet she knew. It was almost as though she had always known but suppressed the thought. One morning as she returned from a shopping trip with Jonathan she decided to tackle him about it and bring things into the open.

Maybe it's partly my fault, she mused when the child was settled into sleep and she was alone with a cup of coffee. I was totally engrossed with motherhood and perhaps he felt pushed out. The baby books warned against this. Yet surely every father who was temporarily overshadowed didn't find another woman?

Who was she? Someone from his office, or someone from the outside world? She knew most of the staff at head office. Not well, but by name and job. She met them at the annual dinner each year. There were some glamorous women working there, yet she would swear that this affair hadn't started more than a few months ago. When they first brought Jonathan home from the nursing home Gordon was still all hers. It was after that things changed. Increasingly they led separate lives.

She poured herself another coffee and thought back to the days when they first met. Her twenty-first birthday party; he was easily the most handsome man in the hall, and the only one she didn't already know. He was invited because he was staying with some friends who were coming and she had included him out of courtesy.

Idly stirring her coffee she recalled every detail of that evening. From the moment when he took her into his arms to dance and the physical thrill that surged through her body. He was the most exciting man she had ever met and they spent a great deal of the evening dancing together.

'You mustn't monopolize me, you know,' she said when he would have danced with her yet again. I must circulate a little now.'

'But I can see you tomorrow, can't I? I return to London next week and — '

'Yes,' she whispered huskily as someone else whisked her onto the floor for the next dance.

On that first date with him she discovered a lively mind that matched her own, and a daring disregard of rules that seemed utterly foolish to them both. He came to Wiltshire to see her every weekend and six months later she moved out of the family home there and into a flat in London. Her parents hadn't approved of the move, although they liked Gordon. She pointed out to them that she could support herself. She had some money of her own now she was twenty-one and in any case she wasn't afraid of working. Her course at the business school when she was eighteen stood her in good stead then, enabling her to find employment in the capital with no difficulty.

She went upstairs to peep at Jonathan. He was still fast asleep. How quickly he was growing up. It didn't seem that long ago since he was a tiny scrap, his incredibly blue eyes gazing at her from the folds of his shawl. Would he flout parental authority too when he was older? She understood her mother's anxiety far better now.

The wedding had been a big affair. Gordon's parents returned from America where his father was on an exchange teacher scheme. Her parents gave them a day to remember, and everything seemed set for a fairytale ending to their courtship and a fairytale beginning to their life together. So where had they gone wrong? Those first two years in London were a whirl of gaiety. Dances, shows, nightclubs, with both of them working and playing hard. Then had come the move to Surrey and the wistful watching of pregnant friends.

When they married she had expected that they would start a family within a few years, and when Gordon was promoted within the international office furniture firm he worked for they bought the house in Richmond and he drove into town every day. That was when they began the eight year fight to have a child of their own. All those hospital visits and consultations, the raised hopes and the desperate disappointment when it didn't happen.

If anyone had told me then that I couldn't have children I wouldn't have believed them, she thought now. I was young and healthy, everything was in my favour, and yet . . . Is it any wonder I went a bit mad when we finally had Jonathan? Yes, maybe I did neglect Gordon a little . . . A cry from upstairs interrupted her reverie and she shook the nostalgic memories from herself and went to fetch her son.

For the first time since his birth her mind wasn't focused solely on him. Even as she played with him and revelled in his smiles and laughter a sliver of her thoughts was trying to unravel who the mystery woman was. She was certain there was one and it was someone he had met since living in Longsands. That didn't rule out people he worked with because she hadn't got to know the ones in Brighton as well as she did the London staff, yet instinct told her this liaison was outside of his job. Apart from anything else she didn't think he would risk jeopardizing that for a fling. That left the gym where he went once a week and the writers' group he also attended weekly. Of course there were other sources but Maureen decided these were the most likely.

'No, Jonathan, don't do that, you'll hurt yourself,' and she scooped her son up and snuggled his head against her shoulder, taking comfort from the soft sweet smell of him.

★   ★   ★

Gordon lay in bed next to Maureen and thought about Katie. Since the first time they had made love, when her husband was away on a course, he had lived for their meetings. Of necessity they didn't happen often, except for the once a week writers' circle. That was a bonus now and he often spent the time there

106

looking at her across the room and weaving his own stories that could never be read aloud to the group. Occasionally they sat together on circle evenings and this meant that he could touch her hand as if by accident and feel the thrill of her response. They were careful not to let this happen too often.

Gordon was in love with Katie in a different way to the first time with Maureen. That had been a meeting of physical and mental needs. A coming together of two minds on the same floor of intelligence and thought.

With Katie it was mostly a physical feeling. His overwhelming desire for her swamped all else. He thought Tim was a fool not to realize what was happening. He knew Katie was often consumed with guilt and he tried to absorb some of this for her sake. But he couldn't. She was so exciting, so vibrant, and if that poor fool of a man she was still in love with, in spite of her passion for himself, couldn't see it, he deserved to lose her.

So far their meetings, apart from the circle which didn't count much because there were always about a dozen others present, had been during the daytime. She even turned down an afternoon job so they could be together and several times a week he took an extended lunch hour and they drove into the country. Once they were disturbed by a group of people searching for wild flowers. Katie was very upset but he managed to gently laugh her out of it. 'Think what a thrill it was for them, my darling. Most of them looked as if they couldn't remember how!'

'Gordon, you shouldn't say such things. It was so embarrassing.'

Taking her in his arms he had kissed her again. 'I bet you were the most beautiful wild flower they've seen today. In any case they have no idea who we are and I do love you so much.'

He thought about her constantly. He and Maureen still slept together in the big double bed, but they had little physical contact. Once he woke up to hear her crying, muffled sobs that shivered through her turned away body.

'Maureen, don't cry, my dear. What is it? Can't you sleep?

'Oh . . . ' She gave up trying to bury her tears in the pillow and let them come noisily. Eventually he turned away, knowing he could offer no comfort that she could accept. He didn't want to hurt her. They had been through a lot together but love had ceased before he met Katie. What was left was a kind of fondness that one might feel for a child.

No, not fondness because what he felt for his child was a powerful protective passion, a love so strong that it was the reason he could never leave Maureen. Jonathan was the bond that held them together. He knew she loved the boy as much as he did and neither of them would ever do anything to hurt or spoil his life in any way. They no longer quarrelled, simply lived in the same house, almost as strangers. Yet, at night Maureen cried herself to sleep and he turned away and tried not to listen.

'Gordon, I need to talk to you,' she said one Saturday afternoon.

'Fire away.'

'It's about Jonathan.'

'What about him He's all right, isn't he. He's not ill or anything? What about him, Maureen?'

'No, of course he's not ill. Sit down, Gordon. I can't hold a proper conversation with you roaming around the room like that.'

He lowered himself into the deep armchair facing her. 'Well?'

'It's not really about Jonathan. It's about us. Oh and him too. It's because of him I want to talk about it.'

He half rose. For a few moments there, panic had risen in him in case something was wrong with the boy. He had seemed rather vulnerable lately; showing off and then bursting into tears when disciplined. Gordon thought it was probably a stage he was going through; feeling his feet, testing them to see how far he could go.

'Please sit down and listen for once, Gordon.' Maureen too looked strained.

He sank back into the velvety depths of the chair. 'There's nothing to discuss about us, Maureen. You know that. I'm — truly sorry,' he added, quickly looking away from the bleakness clearly showing in her face.

'You must have noticed Jonathan's sudden mood changes lately; and the way he works himself into a temper over the silliest little things, and then can't cope with it.'

'It's natural. The child's exploring his feelings, sounding out the world. You can't expect him to 'cope with it'.' He quoted her own words to her as though he were a school-teacher lecturing a child who deliberately misunderstands.

'Can't you see it's because of the way we are? The way we live. He never used to be like this.'

'Nonsense. All children have these tantrums. It's part of growing up.'

'It isn't,' she said passionately. 'Our moods, our — our unhappiness is rubbing off onto Jonathan.'

'What nonsense you're talking, Maureen. He's only a baby still. Certainly not old enough to understand the things that are happening to us.'

'Children, even babies, sense moods. Maybe that's something we lose as we grow older, I don't know. But I do know that we can't go on like this for his sake.'

She softened her voice as she continued, 'I know that you love him as I do and want us to do our best for him. I'm suggesting we either talk this thing through and see if we can't, after all, retrieve something of our marriage.' She paused for perhaps half a second, then said quietly, 'Or I take Jonathan and leave.'

'Leave? Where would you go?'

'Oh, for heaven's sake. I'm not a little Victorian woman who relies on a man for a roof over her head. I'm perfectly capable of earning a living for Jonathan and myself. I have quite a number of skills and I'm not above finding a live-in job until the boy's old enough to start school. You need have no fears that I wouldn't look after him properly. He would not become a 'latchkey kid' as I believe the expression is.'

Gordon had been silent because he was stunned at the turn the conversation had taken. Now he jumped up from the chair quickly and stood facing her. 'I have no doubts as to your efficiency, Maureen. Where does your plan leave me? He is my son too.'

'Oh, Gordon. Let's talk about things. It's only a last ditch plan. I don't want to go.' She raised her head in a gesture of defiance and her voice became strong again. 'For Jonathan's sake, let's try to make our marriage work again.'

They talked until it was time for Maureen to fetch their son from the toddlers' birthday party down the road, and when she had left, Gordon went upstairs to his study. He sat at his desk for some minutes, staring at the silver framed photograph of Maureen and Jonathan taken when the baby first came home from the nursing home. The look of wonder on Maureen's face as she gazed at the child, whose little face peeped from the folds of the soft white shawl she had lovingly knitted, moved him beyond words.

She was right of course. They had drifted, so far and so fast. Why? Was it because of the baby? Certainly it was since the advent of Jonathan. It seemed to him that once she had the child nothing else mattered to her. At first he thought it would wear off, that once she became acclimatized to motherhood everything would slot back into place. It hadn't worked out like that at all. Motherhood had taken over completely.

He had not realized that Maureen knew

about Katie. Not who she was. Not even her name. Simply that there was someone. Women were strange creatures, he thought. A few years ago he couldn't have imagined loving anyone but Maureen. Being physically attracted to another woman, yes; but looking only, not wanting. At least not in the same sense as he now knew he could love, want and need desperately a woman who was going through her own particular hell in her marriage.

And Maureen had known. Even though they no longer shared the kind of life they had once experienced. Even though they'd had little physical contact since trying for Jonathan — she had known. Had sensed this was something serious and she was fighting it viciously.

He heard Maureen's car crunching up the drive. He stood straight and slowly shook himself from his head to his toes. Somehow the movements helped him shake off the first layer of this slough of despair. He put his hands to his eyes and traced his facial features in the way of someone just waking. Then he went downstairs to his wife and son.

12

The telephone was ringing when Maureen entered the house. For a heart-stopping moment when she heard her husband's voice she thought she had lost him. The confrontation over the weekend had been a terrible gamble and had left her feeling shattered.

'I'll be late tonight, Maureen. Don't wait up. A couple of meetings which I must attend, so I'll go straight from work.'

'Isn't it your writers' night?' From somewhere she dredged up a calmness she was far from feeling.

'Yes, it is. I'll try and pop in for a while before I come home. Probably have to give that up. Can't really afford the time.'

His voice sounded hard and the ends of his words were clipped. She knew then that he was fighting to keep his emotions in check. When she replaced the receiver the tears began to fall. So it was someone from that group he was involved with. Maureen had never met anybody from his writers' circle and he had seldom talked about it to her. Was this to be a final farewell or was it to make arrangements for further meetings away from circle nights?

Perhaps it wasn't a woman from that part of his life. After all he met glamorous women frequently in his job. Representatives of foreign countries, smart young career women from all around the British Isles . . .

Brushing away her tears she moved into the kitchen where she had planned to do some baking. With Jonathan at his little friend's house for a couple of hours, and how glad she was that it wasn't her turn to have them both this Monday afternoon, she felt only relief. Give her time to compose herself before Gordon returned.

Strange that it was the boy who had finally brought them together. The child she had yearned for and loved, even to the exclusion of her husband. Surely now, after the weekend's showdown, they could start again. As she crumbled the margarine into the flour, so her thoughts darted about inside her head. Would they be able to recapture a little of the romance of the early years? Or the love they had when Jonathan was a baby? Would she always wonder who the other woman was? Brushing a floury hand across her cheek she let out a deep sigh that seemed to come from the heart of her being.

She loved Gordon, had loved him almost from the first moment they met. Their courtship and wedding really had seemed like a fairytale with him cast as the handsome prince. He had been loving and patient throughout the traumatic childless years — the continual trying for a baby. And, after his initial and natural reticence he had been as joyful as her when their son was born.

Be positive, she told herself. It isn't over yet, but the first round is won. We are still together as a family. Maybe even more of a family than before. Perhaps we can take a holiday, the three of us. A complete change from routine. A fresh start. Yes, that might be a good idea. Make the break with this woman — whoever she is — complete, a thing of the past. Maureen's breath caught on a sob. Damn you, Gordon. We had everything going for us — a nice home, a beautiful child, a reasonable income. What is she like and will you ever completely forget her?

She finished the pastry and tidied herself. Annoyed to find she was trembling as she changed into a clean dress, she poured herself a gin and tonic when she went downstairs again.

'That's better.' Speaking the words aloud gave her confidence. Stupid to think that the last forty-eight hours' events were obvious to others. Yet, as she walked down the road to collect her son, she felt that she was acting a part: the happy wife and mother. She prayed silently that it would soon be true.

*   *   *

Gordon replaced the telephone receiver and sat silently looking at the instrument on his desk. One hurdle over. Now the pattern was set. Tonight he must tell Katie he wouldn't be seeing her again. It was the only way. For a few seconds he thought about writing to her, but he knew he couldn't do it like that. He loved her. Differently to the way he loved Maureen, but truly.

His wife's ultimatum — we sort this thing out between us and make it work, or I take Jonathan and leave you — had shaken him beyond his wildest imagination. They had stayed together for the sake of the boy. They had been through so much to have him, and now, just when he was getting to the age when he enjoyed him even more than when he was a baby, he could lose him.

And Maureen. What of her? During the last forty-eight hours he had relived many memories from the past. But could he get himself together enough to make this retry work? He sat in the chair with his elbows resting on the desk and his interlaced fingers making his knuckles taut. And what about

Katie? God, he loved that woman. Passionately. But she would never leave her husband. Maybe if there was that chance . . . No, he had made his decision last night. 'We'll try again,' he told Maureen.

'And this other woman?' There had been the tiniest catch in her voice as she spoke. It was hardly a break, but he heard it.

'I'll finish it.'

Tonight that must happen. He realized that, initially, he had made all the play, but now it was both of them. They complemented each other, yet both were tied. He didn't think she would ever leave that weak-willed husband of hers. *He's not weak, not really. Just — easygoing.* He smiled grimly to himself as he recalled her saying that, not so very long ago.

There was a knock on his door and, with difficulty, he tried to sound like the efficient businessman he purported to be. When he had dealt with the query he pulled a wire tray filled with letters towards him. If he signed these he could leave early. There wasn't anything else so important that it couldn't wait until morning. Suddenly Gordon needed to be away from the office; out in the air, anywhere except in a closed environment with his thoughts and shattered dreams.

Half an hour later he parked his car on the

cliff top and began walking. His head was filled with Katie. He recalled the first time he had seen her. He remembered her diffidence when she told the circle that she hadn't actually written anything then. Struck immediately by her beauty, he also loved her comic side. Her sense of humour was very much akin to his. *Katie, Katie, how shall I manage without you?*

After a while he sat on the rough grass, closed his eyes and let the images of her take over. Walks across the cliffs, a drive to another town instead of going to circle, an occasional meal in a restaurant when Tim was away or working . . . and the intimate moments, the lovemaking which left him with such tender passion. No, he couldn't face her. Couldn't tell her it was over. It never would be over in his heart. But what of Maureen? She deserved better than this; and Jonathan?

He rose. Brushed himself down and walked on. To think that this time last week they had come up here after circle finished, and made love. Then he had driven her home. Abruptly he turned round and began walking back. He needed to get his thoughts in order.

He went into a pub for a drink and a sandwich before the meeting. Not the one where they sometimes met because he intended to catch Katie before she reached it.

Pulling his wallet from his pocket he took out two photographs. Both were of Jonathan; the one he had shown to Katie in the early days of their acquaintance and one taken just a few weeks ago. He knew well that if Maureen carried out her threat he might never see the boy again. The one thing that held together for them was their love for their son. Surely they could work it out for his sake, if not for what they had once had.

Katie wouldn't have to feel guilty any more either. She might even be relieved that a decision had been taken out of her hands. No, no that wasn't her way. She weighed the pros and cons and made up her own mind. He would miss her so much — what was he going to do? But he had to go through with it if he was to watch and be part of his son's growing up. It had to be a clean break, there was no other choice. His mind wove and dodged about among the images, as though afraid to dwell on any one of them for more than a few seconds. He left most of his sandwich and half of his beer. He put his car in the large car park and walked to the crossroads where he couldn't miss Katie whether she came by bus or walked.

★　★　★

From her seat in the bus Katie saw him waiting and smiled happily. 'Gordon,' she said, when she alighted, 'what a delightful surprise.'

'Can we go somewhere and talk, Katie? It's very important.'

Fear gripped her then. 'Of course. You choose the place.' She noticed then how grim he looked and her first thought was that something had happened to his little boy. He loved that child over and above everything else in the world. Her fingers touched his but there was no answering pressure.

'The car's in the main car park,' he said. She walked by his side silently. Never had she seen him in this kind of mood. It couldn't be because Maureen had found out about her because he *was* here after all. During the last few months she had seen him in many moods, but this — this seeming indifference was quite new. He was striding out more now and she had to walk faster to keep up with him. Opening her mouth to light-heartedly protest in the hope of countering this strange and unusual behaviour she saw the mistiness in his eyes and was quiet.

When they reached the car he unlocked her door and rested his hand softly on her shoulder for a moment as she clambered in. Then he walked round to his side, started the engine and the car moved off. They turned left out of the car park and drove towards the outskirts of the town.

'Where are we going, Gordon? Or is this a mystery tour?'

'I wish to God it was.'

★ ★ ★

Katie was surprised at how calm she was when Gordon told her he and Maureen were going to try again to make their marriage work.

'I loved her once, Katie, and we are a family. For all our sakes I — I'm going back.'

She saw the tears in his eyes and it was as though she was looking in on the scene instead of taking part herself.

'I'll give up the writers' circle,' she said, 'then it won't be embarrassing for you.'

'No, please. You carry on and I'll stop coming. In any case I'm going to be very busy these next few months. I — I'm so sorry, Katie.' His eyes told her he loved her even while his lips were rejecting that love. 'What do you want to do?'

'Go home.' Still she was dry-eyed. Gordon rubbed the back of his hand across his own eyes and she saw the vulnerable muscles in his throat moving. She nearly cried out then.

Part of her was beginning to unfreeze.

'It's the boy, you see. We have to think of our son.'

'Of course you do. Take me home, Gordon.'

She had opened the door and was out of the car as soon as it stopped. Gordon hurried to her side, 'Katie — '

'It's all right. Goodbye, Gordon.'

She took the steps to the front door quickly, fumbled in her bag for the key, knowing all the while that he was there on the pavement watching her. Without looking back she let herself in, closed the door and then leant, trembling, against it.

The tears came when she reached the bedroom. Kicking off her shoes and sprawling across the new pale blue bedspread she cried so much that when she finally rose there was a sopping patch where her face had rested.

'What now?' she asked herself aloud. 'Why didn't he warn me? Give me some indication, however small.' There had been nothing. The last time they had made love, only last week, it had been the best ever.

She looked at her watch. Another hour before Tim would be back from the camp. Katie organized her mind as much as she could. She even congratulated herself on not making a scene. Many women would have.

But I'm not many women, as I once told Tim. I'll survive. I have to.

By the time her husband returned, Katie was in bed and seemed to be asleep. She heard him, and pictured him reading the note she left propped up in the kitchen. *Had a splitting headache so went to bed as soon as I came in.*

When, some little time later, she felt the bed move as he climbed in, she kept very, very still.

'G'night, Katie.' She felt his gentle kiss on her hot forehead and it was very nearly her undoing. As he rolled over to his side of the bed she felt tears pricking beneath her tightly shut eyes, and she pushed the handkerchief she was clutching close to her mouth to muffle any escaping sounds.

13

When Katie missed her next period she tried to tell herself it was because of the trauma she had been through. Since the night Gordon told her they were finished she had busied herself with as much physical work as possible. She resigned from the writing group, giving as an excuse that she was expecting to move shortly and had much packing up to do. She had not become close to anyone there, except Gordon. The rest were simply acquaintances. No one would follow her statement up to keep in touch.

Of course that's what it was. The shock to her system. That afternoon, when Tim had left for the late afternoon/early evening shift and she had the house to herself she suddenly said aloud, 'No, it isn't shock. The most common reason for a missed period is pregnancy. Why should mine be different?' She closed her eyes and for a few moments she recalled that last time. It was only the second time they had not taken any precautions and it was perfect.

'No, no,' she said, 'I'm with child. I'm

expecting Gordon's baby.'

The doctor confirmed her condition a month later. Now she had to tell Tim or Gordon — or both. Her first reaction had been to contact Gordon. For a few hours she imagined how life could be. Then she knew she would never do it.

She told Tim one afternoon when he was on late shift. There was no way that could make it easier for either of them, so she told him starkly and without any preamble.

'Tim, I'm going to have a baby.'

The only thing she refused to tell was the name of the man responsible.

'There's no point, Tim. The — the affair is over and he doesn't know about the baby. I've no intention that he should.'

'What are you going to do then? An abortion?'

Her shocked reaction startled him. 'I couldn't. Surely you know I couldn't. I'd rather it was adopted than that.'

'Yes,' he said.

'No. No, Tim. I want the baby. If, if you could accept it . . . '

He caught hold of her roughly. 'You'd expect me to — '

'Of course not. It was a dream really. A stupid thing to say. Listen, I'll go away. You can tell people whatever you like, Tim, but I'll find a room somewhere and go off. Out of this town.'

'By yourself?'

'By myself. I'll get a live-in job where I can have the baby with me. I don't mind working hard. I've never been afraid of that. But I won't give it up, Tim. I'm sorry as hell about it. Don't think I'm making excuses for myself. I've been a rotten wife in many ways . . .'

She was crying noisily now, unable any longer to control her actions. Tim put both arms round her.

'There you go again, jumping to conclusions. I've got to think about it, Katie. I need time.'

'What is there to think about? It's my problem, but I wanted — wanted you to know how — very — sorry I am, Tim. I — '
She burst into a fresh spasm of sobbing.

★   ★   ★

Tim woke her when he came in from work. It was past midnight and she had only just dropped off into a troubled sleep.

'I've been thinking about things,' he said. 'I've thought of nothing else all night. If you've really finished with this man, and he'll never know about — about your pregnancy,

I'll say the child is mine.'

'Oh, Tim.' She didn't know what else to say. Her gentle, easy-going Tim was going to stand by her. The baby would have a proper home, not a bedsit and a mother who was working in whatever job she could get where she could have an infant with her. She was too choked with emotion to say much so she gave him a loving hug and a rather watery smile. 'I'll make it work, Tim,' she said.

★ ★ ★

The season finished the last week in September. Katie was glad. She had thought, when Gordon left her, that she would need another business for the winter months. To have nothing but the boarding house to decorate wouldn't fill her time enough. Now she knew she could cope with the bleak months with the prospect of Gordon's child at the end of it.

The baby was due in March. Tim said little about her condition after the initial talking, and she had no desire to inflict more pain on him by appearing to gloat. Her dismay and distress when she realized she was expecting were soon replaced by a great joy. After that first child had aroused maternal instincts she had been unaware of, she knew she had to fill herself up with other dreams. Now the dreaming was becoming a reality.

She held imaginary conversations with her husband, speaking words she could not bring herself to say openly, and the child grew within her. When she quickened she longed to mention it to Tim, but life was chugging along so well she was loathe to disturb it. Hugging the thought to herself that her baby was alive and kicking she realized that she hadn't worried in the same way the first time.

At six months she began sorting out names. She broached the subject one evening over their meal.

'I thought Timothy for a boy.'

Keeping her gaze directed downwards onto her plate she said the words quickly and without hesitation. In the silence that followed she sensed Tim had stopped eating, and, slowly she lifted her head and looked across to him.

'That would be nice. What if it's a girl?'

'You choose the girl's name.'

'Sarah,' he said.

Slightly surprised because he hadn't chosen Kate or Catherine she was, neverthe-less, relieved and delighted that he was taking an interest now.

The following month he suggested that she come to the camp where the staff were having a party to celebrate the manager's birthday.

'Well, I'm a bit ungainly,' she said.

'You look bonny. Being pregnant suits you, Katie. And they all know you're expecting a baby in March, anyway.'

'All right.'

She was amazed at the pride he demonstrated. When he had gone to fetch some drinks the man he had introduced as Tony said, 'He's real chuffed about the baby, isn't he, Mrs Bray?'

'I — suppose so, yes.'

Tim returned with the drinks, and another man. 'My wife, Katie,' he said, smiling at her. 'Darling, this is Martin Westtop, tonight's birthday boy.'

She realized, during the evening, that the baby had given him back his pride because his workmates naturally assumed he had fathered the child. Surely that was good. In time the truth of her conception might become so blurred that he would think of it as truly his own. Or was that really living in cloud cuckoo land?

14

Sarah was born on a windy day during the first week of March. Katie woke Tim at three in the morning. 'It's started, Tim. I think I should get to the hospital.' In fact it had 'started' some time before, but she didn't want to disturb his sleep until she really needed to. She judged that time to be now. The pains were getting closer together and she wanted to make sure she was there in time.

Tim didn't stay. 'I have to be at work early tomorrow,' he told a slightly surprised Sister, who was used to husbands hanging about if they brought their wife in at that time of day.

As it happened he would have had to have left before the birth because it was another six hours before the baby arrived.

'It's a girl, Mrs Bray. She's a beautiful baby.'

Katie cuddled the child, and, gazing into her wrinkled face she experienced the strangest feelings. My daughter. My baby. When Sister gently took the yelling infant from her she was reluctant to leave go. 'When can I have her back?' she asked.

'Soon. When she's been weighed and washed. Meanwhile we'll get you back to the ward and you can have a rest.'

'You will bring her back?' she whispered

'Yes, of course.' The kindly Sister touched her hands. 'Don't worry, Mother.'

Katie closed her eyes and lay perfectly still, wondering how they would cope when she was home with baby Sarah. If Tim will cooperate we'll do fine. I just know we will.

Back in the ward she could hear some of the other babies crying, and, opening her eyes, she saw the woman in the next bed lift her child from the crib and talk to it. There was a large white teddy bear sitting on the end of the bed, and the woman said to the baby, 'Your daddy bought you that.'

There and then Katie made a silent vow. That her child would have as much love, as many toys, as much security as anyone in the world. In spite of the circumstances. And if Tim won't help, if he finds it impossible when it really comes down to it, then I will take Sarah and leave. Nothing short of death will separate us now.

Her heart did a rueful leap backwards to how she was just a few years ago; never even guessing at this vast maternal wealth that had been buried inside her until she had that other baby, for such different reasons.

Tim telephoned during the morning and was told he had a daughter. He came in to see them during the evening. He brought her some daffodils, and, after kissing her he sat awkwardly on the chair by the side of the bed.

'Are — are you going to have a look at her, Tim?'

'I suppose so.'

'Go on then. She's in the crib at the foot of my bed.'

He stood up and slowly walked round to see the baby. Katie watched him anxiously, but the only sign was a twitch in the muscles of his face as he gazed at the sleeping child. He sat down and Sister came along.

'You can pick her up, you know. We don't mind.'

Katie quickly came to his rescue. 'Sarah's asleep, Sister. We didn't want to disturb her.'

Tim didn't ask for time off to help Katie when she came home with Sarah. When they asked her at the hospital if she would have someone there for the first few days she said that she would. But in a way she felt relief that Tim wasn't going to be there. She had no visitors booked until the beginning of May, having deliberately not advertised for Easter this time. Sarah would be two months old by then and she knew she could manage.

During her first evening at home John

came downstairs with a present for the baby — a soft, pink elephant. Sarah was asleep in her carrycot and she and Tim were watching television. They had said very little to each other since he came home from work, yet his eyes seemed to be watching her and she had felt glad when he said, 'There's a programme I want to watch. Will it disturb you?'

'No, of course not.' As he walked over to the set to switch it on, she had added softly, 'Sarah will need to get used to it. We won't let a baby disrupt that sort of thing.'

During the off season they used one of the bedrooms on the first floor but kept their large lounge downstairs. Katie went up to the bedroom now and tidied her hair, applied some powder and a touch of lipstick. She was trembling and she told herself not to be so silly. Tim would accept the baby in time. He'd said he would, hadn't he? And surely most men, well a lot of them anyway, were nervous and a bit offhand with a baby at first, even when it was their own.

She patted her cheeks briskly to bring a glow of colour. She allowed herself, for a few seconds, to imagine the scene downstairs. Suppose Tim went to look at the baby while she was gone, and maybe, when she opened the door downstairs she would find him gazing in wonder at the perfection of those tiny features, the softness of that downy black hair — totally opposite to Gordon's fairness. She pulled her thoughts up sharply. Of course he wouldn't. It was going to take time. Time and patience. She uttered a silent prayer that she would have the strength of mind to bear with the situation.

'I know I've not been noted in the past for patience, or any of the attributes I know I need, God, and I know I can't change exactly, but a little help — ' Oh, what's the use, she thought. I can't bargain with God. She clasped her hands tighter together and bowed her head. 'Amen' she said quietly.

When John came in the programme was almost over. They had watched in silence, sitting side by side on the large settee. Did she imagine that Tim moved very slightly as she sat down? She wanted to reach out and touch his hand, but she didn't. Once, as she shifted to make herself more comfortable her arm came close to his cardigan sleeve and she thought she felt him stiffen. Fighting between anger and tears she gazed steadfastly at the screen; at the blurred figures moving about in a drama they knew would have a happy ending. Their own drama was still very much in the balance.

'I just wanted to welcome you home,' John said in his quiet voice, 'and to congratulate you. Here's — here's something for the baby.'

'That's very sweet of you, John. Thank you. She's over there.' He walked over to the carrycot and peered inside. 'What's her name?'

'Sarah. Tim chose it.' As soon as she spoke she realized that it sounded as though she had no say in the matter.

'I — I hope she won't disturb you, John. Though, so far, she's not been a crying baby.' She looked towards her husband.

'You won't hear it up there, anyway,' he said, glancing briefly at their lodger, 'and as long as she doesn't keep me awake when I'm on early shift . . . '

John laughed and she willed Tim to join in but he didn't.

'One of the penalties of being a father, I believe. Anyway I'll go now and leave you in peace. I just wanted to say that I'm glad everything went off well.'

As he moved towards the door Katie said impulsively, 'Thank you for coming in, John, and for Sarah's present. It's really very nice of you and we do appreciate it.'

She waited until she was certain he was out of earshot then she turned on her husband furiously. 'You might have made a bit of effort. D'you want everyone to know you don't care?'

He shrugged. 'Keep your voice down or you'll wake *your* baby up.'

Tears gathered in her eyes and as she squeezed them tightly shut she willed herself not to break down. She took a deep breath and felt them subside. A few moments later she opened her eyes and turned to Tim.

'I'm off to bed,' she said, 'I'm so tired.'

He didn't answer and she couldn't be sure if the very slight movement of his head was supposed to be a nod or the natural sway of his body. She walked over to the carrycot and lifted the baby out. She sensed Tim behind her and, for a moment her heart behaved wildly. She felt it thumping like a hammer as he went past and over to the television set. As she reached the door with Sarah in her arms, Tim returned to the settee, his gaze concentrating now on the programme he had just switched on.

Once upstairs she fed and changed the baby, then put her to bed. She looked so small and vulnerable in the big cot that Katie's tears flowed, and this time she didn't try to quench them.

'Oh, my baby, my darling baby. What have I done?' she cried.

15

Sarah was a happy baby. Katie felt grateful that when the child cried it was usually when Tim wasn't there, almost as though she knew she mustn't upset the delicate balance between them.

For the first few weeks Katie immersed herself in the feel and smell of her baby. Cuddling Sarah and watching her tiny face and exploring hands, Katie felt fulfilled.

Tim came and went. He neither ignored nor acknowledged his wife. He was polite, as a stranger in for a meal might be. When he said, 'thank you' when she passed him the salt or the sugar she wanted to scream at the ordinariness of his attitude. It seemed like a pose.

So, what *do* I want, she asked herself one day when Sarah was asleep and she was ironing Tim's shirt. Would I rather he blew his top, left home, or asked me to leave? She knew he had accepted the baby because it gave him back his masculine pride. She felt bereft that she had killed his love for her.

Sometimes she let thoughts of Gordon intrude. Was he happy now, with his wife and son? Did he ever think about her? Remember their passion? She thought of Sarah as her child and was immensely grateful for her safe and healthy delivery.

'Our summer season will be starting soon,' she said to Tim one evening. 'I thought I'd move our bedroom back downstairs next week, in readiness.'

'Leave it 'til Sunday and I'll help you. You're not strong enough yet.'

When she took the baby upstairs to bed she cradled her gently and whispered, 'Oh, Sarah. He almost sounded like the old Tim this evening. Maybe everything will be all right eventually. As you grow perhaps we shall, after all, become a happy family.' The baby gurgled contentedly.

Katie lay in bed, daring to dream and when Tim came up later and climbed into bed beside her she snuggled close to him. He rolled over so his back was towards her.

'Goodnight, Katie,' he said.

She squeezed her eyes tightly together and forced her tears to stay inside.

During the summer she watched Sarah's progress with lonely delight. When one of the visitors said, 'She's a lovely baby, Mrs Bray, you and your husband must be so proud of her,' she thought what a stupid remark it was. Yet, how many times had it been said to parents the world over? How many times was it not relevant? In this case it was not even true because Tim took scarcely any notice of Sarah and her natural father was unaware of her existence.

Katie worked hard that summer and was glad she had so much to do. She kept scrupulous accounts for the boarding house and always paid for Sarah's clothes and needs with this money. It hurt that Tim had not once bought the baby anything. When, one day he brought in a beautiful doll, her heart soared with happiness. His words, however, soon battered her hopes to the ground.

'The chaps and girls at work clubbed together and sent it for the baby.' Fighting her disappointment she said, 'It's — it's lovely, Tim. Why don't you give it to her.'

Sarah was in the carrycot and she stood aside to let him pass, but he thrust the doll into her arms and hurried out. Her tears dripped onto the doll's pink dress and she hastily brushed her hand across her eyes. It was no use moaning. Why should Tim feel anything for the baby? For either of them now, and yet, for a while during the waiting time, although she realized the reasons for his behaviour, she had hoped.

John moved on during the summer. 'My firm are opening a new branch and want me to manage it, Mrs Bray. I'll miss Longsands, and you and Mr Bray, but it would be foolish to refuse.'

'Of course, John. We shall miss you, though. You've been with us a long time. Our very first guest.' She smiled at him, knowing it was true that she would miss him even if Tim didn't. 'Where will you be going?'

'Mately, in Kent. It seems a pleasant place. A small market town. I'm going down this weekend to sort out somewhere to live.'

She left John's room spare during the rest of the summer and had decorators in when the season finished.

'I thought we could turn it into a nursery for Sarah,' she said to Tim one evening when they were both in together. These occasions seemed to happen less and less frequently now, but she had given up mentioning the fact. The guests and her daughter kept her busy enough, although in her more depressive moments she wondered how long she would stay. Perhaps it would be best to move on herself and admit her marriage was over. They no longer fought as they had in the early days in the flat, but the silences were more sinister. At first Katie tried, but lately even she had given up dreaming that one day they would be happy again.

Her joy in Sarah was the shining light in

her life. She had never thought of herself as a maternal woman, and, until she had borne that first child she had not known, nor even guessed at the depth of love within herself. She thought of that little boy and wondered if he had given the other woman and her husband the happiness Sarah had brought to her. *I hope so; yes, I really do hope so.*

She knew she would never do anything like that again, for any reason. It was as though a previously untapped spring within her had been released. It made her mentally and physically shudder now when she thought about what she did and why. Especially why. Yet two people, who presumably couldn't have a child on their own, had been given the chance to become a family through it and she felt good about that aspect.

She seldom allowed her thoughts to stay with Gordon, but on the rare occasions when she did she was ashamed that she had succumbed so quickly and so easily.

I did love him and he loved me. But was it because we were both in trouble with our true loves? He excited me, he made me feel all woman. In her mind she heard his voice — that voice she had thrilled to over all those mad months. *Yet in the end, while I was still at the height of my passion, he left me.* His wife won. As Tim had always won in her heart, for she never had any intention of leaving him. Not then, not ever. Or would she have done when she became pregnant if Gordon had not already gone by then? Trying hard to be truthful to herself, Katie acknowledged that, in those circumstances she probably would have done.

Sarah stirred in her cot and Katie stood looking down at her. The fluffy dark hair of her first few days had soon rubbed off and when it had grown again it was fair like Gordon's. That was the only likeness she could see, the colour of her daughter's hair, and it wasn't an unusual shade, there were dozens of babies with the same colour. The shape of her nose and mouth and the set of her eyes were the image of Katie's.

Now her hair was slightly damp where she had sweated; the incredibly long, golden eyelashes were in a curve and casting a delicate shadow on her cheeks. The soft pink lips and smooth baby skin were so perfect Katie felt a huge lump rise in her throat. Oh, my darling, she thought, I do love you. Sometimes I know I don't deserve you, but I do love you so much, so very much.

Sarah moved into the nursery just before Christmas. Now decorated in pale pink and with a brightly coloured animal frieze around the walls and teddy bears on the curtains, it

143

was a very pretty room. She asked Tim to come and see it.

'Well, what do you think?' Her voice was low, anxious.

'It's okay.' After a pause he added, 'It looks very feminine.'

As he turned to go she said, 'It will be nice to have our room to ourselves again, won't it, Tim?'

'Makes no difference to me.'

'No, it doesn't, does it? Nothing makes any difference to you these days. For crying out loud, you accepted the child, Tim. You said we'd stay together. I would have left. I would have taken Sarah and gone, but you wanted me to stay. You — '

'I have accepted the child. Everyone thinks she's mine. What more do you want?'

'What more, what more?' She knew her voice was at screaming pitch, but suddenly she had to let fly. She had held herself in for too long in the hope of a proper reconciliation.

'A normal married life. That's what more. And you haven't accepted the child, Tim. You refer to her as my baby, when you refer to her at all. But don't worry, we won't go on like it much longer because I'll go. I'll look for a live-in job and Sarah and I will move out after Christmas.'

The baby, downstairs in her playpen, started crying, and Katie brushed past her husband and hurried to her.

Tim went out shortly afterwards and Katie took Sarah into the newly decorated room and gazed around it with tears of frustration and anger in her eyes.

They made up almost as they used to. Tim brought her back a box of chocolates and said he was sorry they'd quarrelled.

'And I suppose you think everything's all right now? Well, it isn't, Tim. We need to sort out where we go from here. I accept full responsibility for the state we're in, but — but I can't patch us up alone. Tim, look at me, darling, please.'

'All right, Katie.' She saw he was steeling himself for a showdown. Knowing how much he hated arguments she felt a great surge of compassion. They had loved each other once. She still loved him and she thought he loved her; that there was still a glimmer of his feelings beneath the hurt which she had inflicted.

'Tell me whose child she is,' he said. His voice was as bleak as his face.

'I can't do that.'

'Can't? Or won't?'

'All right, won't. Because it wouldn't be fair to anyone. It was over and finished before

145

Sarah was born and no good can possibly come of you knowing the man's name, Tim.'

'It was John, wasn't it, and that's why he's moved out? Why you're suddenly so anxious to leave after Christmas. I suppose he's settled in this new job now and has found somewhere for you all to live. Very convenient. Poor old Tim can provide shelter until we work something out. Poor old Tim'll go along with it. He can't father a child himself, but he'll not turn out the one his wife's lover's created . . . ' his voice became tangled with sobs and he turned and rushed from the room.

Stunned into silence, all the fire went from her temper, then, suddenly she seemed to come alive again. Tears pouring down her cheeks she ran after her husband.

'Tim, it wasn't John. Oh, my dear, did you really think that? Here in our own home? Tim, it was someone I met at the writers' circle. He never knew about the baby. The affair was already over. It should never have happened, Tim, but I was so unhappy and I stupidly — '

'What was his name?'

'What good would it do if you knew? He was married. We were both married. Oh Tim, I know we can't wipe it out, but we — we could start again if — if you have any kind of

146

feeling left for me. If not,' her natural independence rose again, 'if not, then Sarah and I will leave. And I promise you we shall not be going to her father, nor to any man.'

16

Sarah was two years old when Katie was rushed into hospital. She had been feeling unwell for several months, and she was already booked in for an appointment with the specialist there. A massive haemorrhage one evening when she came downstairs after settling her daughter for the night bypassed that appointment.

Tim unlocked the front door on returning from work in time to see her clutch the newel post at the foot of the stairs. She seemed to crumple as she fell almost at his feet. He went in the ambulance with her, at the last moment remembering Sarah and calling on Mrs Jones next door to ask her to sit with the child.

In the waiting room in the hospital he found himself praying. *Dear God, will she be all right? Please let her be all right.* It seemed a long time before they came to tell him he could see his wife. She was lying very still, and her face, above the crisp white fold-back of the sheet was jaundiced in comparison. Attached to one arm were tubes which were connected to two bottles. One contained clear liquid and one contained blood. She was conscious and she smiled at him. That nearly broke his heart.

'Tim. I'm sorry,' she said.

'Whatever for? Don't worry, just get well, Katie.'

Awkwardly he touched her cheek and she fumbled to bring her free hand from beneath the tightly tucked in bedclothes. Desperately trying to find some comforting words for her, he said, 'Sarah's fine. I asked Mrs Jones next door to stay with her.'

Her tears overflowed then and she pulled her hand away to rub at her eyes. 'Thank you, Tim. Look after her, please. I've got to have an operation . . . '

Sister suddenly appeared by his side. 'Time's up I'm afraid, Mr Bray.' He leant over the bed and gently kissed Katie's cheek.

'It'll be all right,' he said. 'Just get better, darling.' He saw the doctor before leaving the hospital.

'We will operate as soon as she is fit enough. We are giving her blood now. Telephone in the morning to see how she is.'

He heard his voice saying thank you to the doctor, and then he was walking down the stairs, the vision of Katie lying in that high hospital bed, vivid in his mind.

It wasn't until Mrs Jones had left, after

promising to look after Sarah while he was at work, that he thought seriously about the little girl. Since their reconciliation he still had taken hardly any notice of her. Often she was already in bed when he returned from work, and in this period between Christmas and Easter it was almost all daytime work. The only shifts had been during the four-day Christmas holidays when the camp had a 'special' on the go. This was something they did every year for a group of disabled children from two day centres in Brighton. Katie and Sarah had come to the camp on Boxing Day and taken part in the activities. He had been busy and not seen very much of them even then.

He went into the little girl the next morning. 'Sarah, mummy's had to go away for a few days, so we must look after each other. I'll have to go to work later, but I'll be back tonight, so — so Mrs Jones next door is going to look after you. You know Mrs Jones, don't you?'

The child looked back at him, her eyes solemn in an unsmiling face. She was sitting up in her cot, a half undressed doll in her hands. Tim walked closer and let the side of the cot down.

'Come along, then. We had better get you washed and dressed.'

The child returned her attention to the doll and continued putting the clothes on it. Tim leant over and lifted her out.

'Want my dolly,' she shouted, and then, her eyes filling with tears, 'Want Mummy, want Mummy. Mummy, Mummy, Mummy . . . '

'Oh God. Listen, Sarah . . . ' Frantically he tried to soothe her, but it was no use. He carried her, kicking and struggling, into the bathroom, took off her pyjamas and nappy, and then attempted to wash her. As soon as he stood her down without holding her she ran off. The more he tried to stop her crying the louder she screamed. He didn't know what to do.

'Sarah, come on now. Where are your clothes?' Back in the nursery he opened a drawer in the little chest and found a jumper and a pair of check trousers. With one hand still restraining the screaming child he reached for a nappy from a contraption hanging above the chest of drawers.

'You'd better lay down,' he said, then louder and very crossly, 'Sarah, stop this noise this minute and lay on the floor.' Whether it was the sharpness of his tone or the surprise in his change of attitude he didn't know, but the yelling stopped and she lay on the floor with her legs in the air. Taking advantage of the sudden lull, he pulled the nappy open. Wonder how these things go. Should have noticed when I took the other one off.

Sarah, realizing what he was doing, sat up. 'Knickers,' she said, 'no nappy.'

'Yes, nappy.'

'No nappy. Not bedtime, no nappy,' the noise began again, and only his hold on her stopped her from racing off. After the second attempt when she pulled not only the sticky bits at the side, but some of the stuffing from the disposable nappy did it dawn on him that the poor child thought she was being put back to bed.

'Sarah, it's all right. I understand now. You wear knickers in the daytime. Come on, love. Show me where they are.' Eventually he had her dressed. Better give her something to eat now, he thought. And ring the camp and tell them I'll be late. At that moment the front doorbell rang and Mrs Jones called out, 'Mr Bray, it's only me.'

Holding the struggling child in his arms he went to the door. 'I was just going to give Sarah her breakfast.'

The tearful child and harassed looking man told Mrs Jones all she needed. 'I'll do it if you like. I expect you have to be at work soon. Just leave me the key and I'll sort things out.' She took Sarah from him and stood her down, holding tightly to her hand.

'Come along, pet, you can help me find everything and we'll let Daddy get off, shall we?'

'Mummy, Mummy, Mummy, want Mummy . . . '

'Of course you do. We'll sort that one out too, but first, let's have something to eat and clear up, shall we?' Picking the struggling little girl up again she went indoors.

'Don't worry, Mr Bray. She'll soon get over it. I expect she's a bit frightened, but she'll be okay when you get back. What time will it be, just roughly?'

A quarter of an hour later Tim had shaved, grabbed a quick cup of tea and marvelled at the tranquillity in the kitchen, where Sarah was strapped into her highchair with a fistful of bread and marmite.

★ ★ ★

Katie woke in the night and wondered where she was. There was a dim light burning and she felt terribly weak. Trying to turn over she pulled at the tubes attached to her arm. Someone said softly, 'Everything's all right, Mrs Bray. Just lay still and rest a while longer.'

Then she remembered. 'Have I had an operation, nurse?'

'Not yet.'

Katie was in hospital for two weeks before they operated. For the first week she was very ill indeed, but the blood transfusions gave her back her fighting spirit. Every night Tim came in straight from work and sat with her for half an hour. Then he left to collect Sarah from Mrs Jones.

'She's fine,' he said, in answer to her queries, 'and Mrs Jones is an angel in disguise, Katie. She looks after her all day and I take over at night.'

He didn't tell her that for the first week Sarah had screamed for two hours after going to bed. That he had sat by the cot and talked to her, told her stories, taken her out and attempted to cuddle her, until she had finally fallen asleep exhausted. She still cried for Katie at bedtime, but he could distract her easier now, and she no longer screamed in frightened panic.

After two weeks in hospital the doctor told Katie they were ready to operate.

'A hysterectomy is a standard operation, Mrs Bray, and you are so much stronger now than you were. You do understand that it will mean no more children, don't you?'

Katie lowered her head and avoided his gaze. 'Yes, I know, doctor.'

'I would like to speak to your husband also

when he visits this evening.'

Katie felt a surge of fear within her, but she knew that the doctor would speak to Tim whatever she said. He was late coming in. The last of the tubes had been detached several days previously and she sat up in bed and watched the door. She would know by his face if the doctor had already seen him. As he approached her bed she saw that he had.

'Everything all right, Tim?'

'Of course. Why wouldn't it be?'

'No reason. Just that it's such a lot for you to do. Working and looking after Sarah and, and everything. But not for much longer,' she rushed on, 'they're going to operate on me within a few days now and then I can start looking forward to coming home. Oh Tim, Tim, I do so badly want to come home.' To her dismay she began to cry and he put his arm round her very gently.

'Katie, it's okay. Stop worrying.'

'Sorry.' She sniffed and he suddenly smiled at her. When he did that the dark, closed look left his face and, for a few seconds he seemed to be the boyish, easy-going Tim he had been before.

'I saw the doctor tonight,' he said. 'He seems confident that once this is over you'll feel better than you have for some time.'

'What — what else did he say?'

'You know damn well. That there would be no more children.'

Her lips trembled, and although she tried to speak, nothing came out.

'Stop torturing yourself, Katie. Just get well and come back home to us.'

She was still crying when he left. Sister had come over and pulled the curtain round her bed. Then she had suggested that Tim go while they settled his wife down.

'Now, Mrs Bray, what is the matter? Did you and your husband quarrel? You can tell me you know, because I may be able to help. I too have had a hysterectomy and my husband was hoping for a large family. I know it isn't always easy when you are still of child-bearing years, but, my dear, you have one child. I had none.'

In the midst of her sobs the Sister's words came through to her and she wanted to laugh. But the crying was stronger than the laughter. Instead, she heard herself saying in an odd, catchy voice that didn't sound like hers at all, 'It's just retribution, that's what it is, just retribution. I'll be all right in a minute, Sister, really I will . . . '

She couldn't find the words to tell her that she was also crying because Tim had said, 'come home to *us*.'

★ ★ ★

During Katie's stay in hospital Tim and Sarah became friends. The first two weeks were hell. Mrs Jones told him what a good child she was. 'Of course she misses her mother, poor little mite, but she's an absolute darling.'

Once his neighbour had left the 'little darling' turned into a bad tempered little girl. She shouted, she screamed, she refused to cooperate in any way, and he simply didn't know what to do. Tired and worried, he struggled on, eventually getting her into her cot, where she stood and rattled the sides, often trying to climb out, and all the while crying and screaming with temper.

It was when the screaming turned to sobs, genuine heartbreaking sobs, that he felt sorrier for her than for himself. How could he explain to a two-year-old what was happening? Her mother had put her to bed one evening and the child hadn't seen her again and was being looked after by people she didn't know well. He thought of taking her to the hospital with him but was afraid to in case that made matters worse. It would upset Katie to see her like that too, and Sarah would undoubtedly cry when she had to leave. The hospital might not let her in anyway. From a practical point of view it was easier not to take her, then he could visit straight from work.

He spoke the truth when he told Katie how marvellous Mrs Jones was being to them. At the camp, when he told them his wife was in hospital, the manager changed his shifts so he was on daytime only for a while. He also suggested that he bring the baby to work with him if he couldn't find anyone to look after her.

'There's the nursery, and she would have the advantage of you being on the premises and able to look in from time to time.'

Tim thanked him, but declined the offer while his neighbour was willing to do the job. Fleetingly he wondered what his colleagues would think of a father whose child screamed and kicked every time he went near her.

The turning point came when he fell asleep one evening while trying to console Sarah. He had been reading one of her picture books to her. He had put the cot side up to prevent her from climbing over, and was reading the story and showing her the pictures through the bars. Sarah was taking no notice. All her concentration was on getting out. He had learned not to try and stop her screaming — it wasn't possible anyway, but he thought that if he was there, trying to play with her, then perhaps she wouldn't feel so lonely.

It had been a hard day at the camp. Redecorations for Easter, in which all of them had taken part, then the dash to the hospital to visit Katie on the eve of her operation. The previous night he had slept little, and as Sarah quietened down a bit he felt himself several times almost dropping off into slumber. Each time he conquered it, turned a page and tried to interest and tire the child even more so that she would fall asleep and he could tuck her in and relax. Instead he fell asleep.

When he woke it was dark. Sarah was talking in nonsense language and playing with his hands through the bars. He felt stiff and hungry, but immediately aware of a new feeling between this little girl and himself.

'Sarah,' he whispered softly, 'go to sleep now. It's very late. I'll see you in the morning.'

His eyes were focusing in the dark now. It wasn't completely black; the moonlight filtered through the nursery curtains and gave a gentle glow to the room. Reaching over the top of the cot he wriggled the child down beneath the covers, stood and watched her for a moment as she sighed, put two fingers in her mouth, and then appeared to go right off to sleep.

The following morning she greeted him with a smile. 'Hello,' she said, 'read book.'

'Tonight, Sarah. I have to go to work now, but tonight when I come home, I'll read the book to you.'

He let the sides of the cot down and reached in. For the first time the little girl lifted her arms and cooperated.

When he rang the hospital during the afternoon Katie was still in the recovery room. He went back to work and telephoned again just before leaving for home.

'She's comfortable,' Sister said.

Sarah greeted him like an old friend. It was as though the child had been testing him. Or did she think, in her little two-year-old mind, that her mother had deserted her? That she would have to make do with him now? What did children think when things happened that were temporarily beyond their comprehension?

★   ★   ★

Katie was away for six weeks. It should have been two but the day before she was due home she developed an infection. It didn't respond to the antibiotics and she became very ill indeed. Tim took time off work to sit with her during the most critical stages. Although she seemed to be asleep most of the time, he thought she knew he was there, and he hoped it comforted her. He returned

160

home each night because of Sarah.

Thinking about his marriage during the small hours when he couldn't sleep he usually went into the kitchen to make some tea, but he always looked in on Sarah first. He'd lean over and tuck her in, sometimes stroking her cheek softly with his finger. Occasionally she would sigh, or turn slightly, but mostly she lay still and beautiful with sleep.

One night he took his tea into the nursery and sat on the little chair, watching her. Whose child was she? Did it matter any more? To all intents and purposes she was theirs now — his and Katie's. He had even chosen her name. Strangely he had not had to think about it when Katie asked him. He had always thought Sarah was a beautiful name, and now, since growing to love the child so very much he was glad that it had been his choice. Sitting by her cot Tim began to make plans for the little girl's future.

The next morning when he telephoned the hospital the news was good. Katie was going to recover. He bought a large bouquet of flowers to take in with him that evening.

She was sitting up in bed, her hair a curtain of rich brown around her shoulders.

'I'll soon be home now,' she told him. 'It seems as if I've been here forever. How long is it, Tim?'

'Nearly six weeks.'

Suddenly she clutched his hand fiercely. 'How is Sarah? Oh I know you've said she's fine, but, but Tim, I've not seen her for so long. Is she really all right? It — it must have been awful for you.'

'She is really all right, Katie, honestly. And no, it hasn't been awful, not that part of it. Only you being so ill. That's been my nightmare. Sarah and I — well, we're friends now — we've,' he swallowed hard, 'we've got to know each other and I love her too now, Katie. In fact I was thinking, only the other night, that maybe I could — could officially adopt her . . . Oh, darling, don't cry please. I won't if you don't want me to.'

'Tim.' Katie's voice came from her throat on the tremble she felt inside her. 'I never expected that. That you accept her is happiness enough. That you want to adopt her, what a bonus.'

'Hush, darling, please. Sister will say I'm upsetting you. We'll talk about it when you're home and stronger. I do love you, Katie.'

★ ★ ★

Sarah was shy with her mother when she returned home. She turned to Tim whenever she wanted anything, and Katie fought back her tears. Tim was gentle with the little girl, gentle but firm. He stayed home for the first few days, then he returned to work, and she was glad to see him go.

I'm jealous, she thought. Jealous of Sarah's friendship with Tim. It's ridiculous because it's what I wanted, what I prayed for. But then I didn't realize she would love him instead of me. I thought it would be as well as me.

It was June before she opened the boarding house again, and by then she was very much stronger. Tim insisted on her having help and Mrs Sandley joined them a few days before the first visitors arrived. By then she and Sarah were back on the old footing of mother and daughter, but with the added joy of Tim taking his place and both giving and receiving love from what he jokingly called, 'both my women'.

They had a party for her birthday. Katie made and iced a sponge cake and two little girls who lived down the road, and a brother and sister who were a little bit older and lived opposite, came to tea. They did it on the Sunday when Tim was off for the afternoon and it went fairly well. Only one dodgy moment during tea, which they had sitting on cushions on the floor with a big plastic tablecloth spread in front of them. The little boy pushed his sister and she fell against the child next to her who had just spooned some jelly into her mouth. She screamed and threw the spoon at her, and suddenly jelly and spoons seemed to be flying everywhere. It only lasted a few seconds, before Katie and Tim had them sorted, removed the rest of the jelly and brought forward the drinks. By then Sarah was laughing delightedly with the little boy, who obviously thought he had made a conquest there and was ready to follow it up. Tim forestalled him from tipping the contents of his plastic tumbler over his poor sister, which earned him a sullen look from the culprit and a grateful one from Katie.

'Whew,' Katie said later when she had tucked up a tired but happy child, 'I didn't know a small children's party could be so dangerous.'

17

'Move, Katie? Whatever for? There's nothing wrong with this place, and since we've taken over a few more rooms for ourselves, it's very comfortable indeed.'

'I know. But there's this lovely house at the other end of town. I saw a picture of it in an estate agent's window the other day and it's been in my mind ever since.'

They were sitting opposite each other eating their evening meal. Sarah was upstairs in the little bed they had bought for her last year, and Katie hoped she had picked her moment well. She knew Tim would fight against it and she had her arguments ready.

'There's a paddock, so Sarah could have a pony, a beautiful conservatory, Tim, and a fair-sized garden. You wouldn't need to do anything to it because it would be something for me to do when I give up the guest house. You've wanted me to ever since my operation, haven't you? But I need something, darling. Especially when Sarah starts school next year, and I'm fit enough now. I've always hankered after a really nice garden. Tim, just think. All our own vegetables and masses of flowers, and in the conservatory we could grow more exotic plants. At least come and look at it Tim. Please. I'm sure you'll love it.'

'We're settled here. This house suits us and we don't need to move for you to give up the guests. Anyway, we've got a garden here,' he added as she went to speak.

'But not as large as that one. Nothing like. In any case most of ours is concrete for carparking. Be fair, Tim, we can't do very much with that bit at the end now, can we?'

'I didn't know you wanted a huge garden, Katie.'

Spearing a piece of roast potato with her fork she said quietly, 'There are too many bedrooms here for us, Tim, if we don't take guests.'

'How many in this grand place then? Doesn't sound like a two up, two down property.'

She laughed softly, aware how brittle the ground she was treading was. 'It only has three bedrooms. Which could be one for us, one for Sarah, and a spare for visitors.'

'Have you looked over this place?'

'No. I've simply seen a picture of it in an estate agent's window and read the bumph. I didn't even go in and get the full details. But it wouldn't hurt to look at it, would it now?'

Tim shrugged his shoulders. 'What's for pudding?' he said.

Katie went to see Garice House three days later. Neither of them had mentioned it since, but she had thought of scarcely anything else. If she did the preliminaries, and if she found the place would be worthwhile, then she felt sure Tim would take a look. They had a healthy bank balance now and were sure to be able to sell their present home at a profit. Because they had bought cheaply and kept the property up, they could come out of the deal with a handsome sum to bank. Katie felt a thrill as she contemplated the idea. The estate agent's particulars were safely in her handbag and at least once each day, when Tim was at work and Sarah happily occupied, she had taken them out and re-read them.

Detached house situated in pleasant area in Rosedale Gardens. The property consists of spacious hall, two reception rooms, three bedrooms (one ensuite), fitted kitchen, bathroom, large utility room, conservatory. Quarter of an acre garden, paddock, summer-house, garden shed and garage.

It sounded great, and would be the first one where there were not things to be done, she thought. At least that's how it looked to be on paper, but she would keep an open mind. She consulted a map of Longsands and

167

found it was situated to the west of the town. The local buses served the area and there was a school and a church not too far away.

Katie declined the estate agent's offer to take her along to view the house, but asked him to make an appointment for her to do so and she and Sarah set off to walk into town for the bus; it was a twenty minute bus ride. Rosedale Gardens looked quietly respectable. It was a ten minute walk from the bus stop and Katie made a mental note to check the prices of second hand cars. That would be better for Tim and they would be able to use it to go further afield on his days off as well. In answer to Sarah's, 'Where we going, Mummy?' she said, 'To visit a lady's house. It won't take long and we'll buy an ice cream to eat on the way home.'

Katie fell in love with the house the moment she stepped into the elegant hall. It was large enough to be a room — furnished with a velvet covered chair, two small round tables, each holding a magnificent blooming plant, a beautiful dark oak chest and a clover fitted carpet that tingled of luxury as soon as your feet touched it. The rest of the rooms lived up to their descriptions. The conservatory surpassed her expectations, although she realized that it was probably because of the wonderful 'garden' the present owners had created there. Katie knew that she too would bloom in such surroundings.

Upstairs was equally satisfying; the oyster satin wallpaper in the main bedroom making her long to touch it, to run her hand along its richness. She did no such thing of course, and, when Sarah spied a delicate pastel china lady and cried out in delight, 'Oh look, Mummy. Isn't she pretty? She's like ours Daddy won at the fair,' for the first time in her life Katie wanted to smack her little daughter. She saw the amusement in the woman's eyes, and forced herself to smile back and say, 'She means the one in her room which she had so set her heart on.'

The garden was lovely: two lawns, several flower beds, shrubs, trees, and, through a rustic archway, a kitchen garden. The paddock was empty.

'We've already sold the horses. We are going abroad which is why the price includes carpets and curtains.'

When they were walking back to the bus stop Sarah tugged at her hand. 'Why did we go there, Mummy? She had no children for me to play with.'

It took a long time to persuade Tim to even look at Garice House. 'It's far too much money, Katie. You're paying for the area, that's all. The posh end of town. It's where

169

you've always wanted to be, isn't it? All through the years none of this has been good enough for you. Right from that first flat, they've all been stepping stones to this. And what would we have left? Nothing. By the time — '

'But we would, Tim. We'd get a good price for this place. All these rooms, in a good position, well decorated, anyone could move in without doing a thing to it. We're not just selling a house, we're selling a business. A potential one if we don't accept any bookings and one with goodwill and an income if we do. Another thing Tim, have you noticed, it's getting very rowdy round here, small gangs hanging around rather menacingly. So far they are only standing about and staring but look what's happening in Brighton and other big towns. It could spread here. Tim, please don't turn it down without thinking about it. It will be the prize at the end of the line, darling. No more visitors invading our privacy, a tastefully and beautifully decorated house — '

'I've seen nothing wrong with the way you've decorated and furnished this place, Katie. For goodness' sake be honest with me. You want this house because it's what you've dreamed of for years. It's what you — ' He hesitated, then plunged on, 'What you almost left me for, way back.'

Katie had learned when to leave things be. She often thought of that first child, the baby she should never have held in her arms. Would the ache be even worse if she hadn't held him? Her thoughts didn't anguish her now as they once had, but given the time again she knew she wouldn't do it, no matter how much money she was offered.

Sometimes, not often, she thought about Gordon. That love had given her Sarah. She loved her daughter with the fervour of a woman who has loved and lost before. The miracle was that now, since her illness, Tim also loved Sarah as though she were his own. He had even talked of adopting her officially, but because his name was on the birth certificate as her father anyway it seemed best to let it stay and not create waves. Better for them all, especially for Sarah.

It was because of Sarah that he eventually agreed to move to Rosedale Gardens. 'She shall have a pony and dancing lessons and — and things like that, Katie, if she wants them. Have you thought that she might not? She may decide to be a racing driver.' His eyes twinkled at her now. 'Her career, when the time comes, must be her choice, not something to please us. Right?'

'Of course, Tim.'

His next words made her realize that she didn't know her husband as well as she thought she did.

'I shall leave the holiday camp.'

'Leave! But what will you do, Tim?'

'Get another job of course. Something more in keeping with the new address, and, more to the point, something that will ensure that we can keep up the payments.'

'But . . . ' She saw his eyes were laughing at her. 'Tim Bray, you've already done it, haven't you? Well?'

'Not quite. But I've set the action going. Suzanna's, that new restaurant on the hill, asked me some time ago to be the catering manager. I telephoned the owner yesterday to ask for an appointment.'

A pain went through Katie's body. Was it jealousy? she wondered. Tim was actually going to change his job. Not for her, but for Sarah. And they were going to live in that lovely house. It was only a few miles in measurable distance but how many more in achievement?

Of course they first had to find a buyer for their present house, but she had no doubts that they would, and get a good price too. Yes, they had come a long, long way from that grotty little flat after all.

Aware that Tim was speaking, she turned

to face him again.

'It's the last time though, Katie. As high as I want to go. No mansions. I've no desire to live in Buck House.'

'Tim, of course not. I reckon this will do us fine.' She tried to sound lighthearted, but the look on his face was such as she had never seen before.

'One other thing. If you want to move again, you go alone. And I mean alone. Because I shall stay put and Sarah will stay with me. No one will dispute the right because my name is on her birth certificate as her father.'

★ ★ ★

Tim gave a month's notice to the holiday camp, 'because I've been there so long and I don't want to let them down,' he told Katie.

'You have never let anyone down in your life, Tim. You deserve this job, you really do. Sometimes I'm still amazed that you went for it. Suzanna's is a lovely restaurant. I walked past the other day.'

He grinned at her. 'It seats sixty and they have a huge function room at the back.'

'If the food's as good as the décor it will do fine. I love those royal blue carpets and pretty lampshades on the walls by the tables.'

'Well, they've a very good chef, and, until now, the owner has been managing the place himself. He's built the reputation but he doesn't want to be tied, so I shall be the first catering manager. I hope it will work out well. I've never had so much responsibility before.'

Katie slipped her arm through his. 'You'll be a great catering manager, Tim. You should have done something like this years ago instead of slogging away in the camp.'

'You could be just a little bit prejudiced,' he joked.

The boarding house sold quickly and for a good price. 'I knew it would,' Katie said jubilantly, 'maybe we should have asked more.'

Tim shook his head, 'I thought we'd have to drop the price. I'm pleasantly surprised.'

She wrote to John to give him the new address and he telephoned to say that he would be down to see them once they had settled in. 'And may I bring someone with me?'

'Of course,' Katie said.

'It's a girl. We got engaged last week on her birthday.'

★ ★ ★

The first flush of excitement about the Rosedale Gardens house had faded. The

174

happiness was still there, but with it came a nagging feeling that she had to make it right for Tim. Never had she seen him more adamant about anything than when he had told her, 'It's the last time. If you want to move again you go alone. Without Sarah or me'.

Sarah was four now and attending a nursery school in town. Katie saw no reason to transfer her to a nearer one. After all, she would be starting at the big school within a year, and it would be no hardship to take her into town each morning. I can shop, browse around the antique shops, pop in to see old George Pugh. Might be able to pick up a few nice pieces, though I shall have to watch the spending for a bit with this much higher mortgage.

She hadn't said anything yet to Tim, but she still toyed with the idea of buying a second hand car. If Tim had been staying at the holiday camp it would have been useful because of the distance and the odd hours, but he would still need transport to get to his new post at Suzanna's. The bus did go close, but they were less frequent at night when he would be finishing work. Not yet, she decided. It will be a nice walk in the summer and there are buses, but maybe in the winter. After all we aren't really hard up now, with what I've saved over the years from the letting, and Tim's new position with a much higher salary. I may find myself a little job too, once Sarah is at proper school.

Meanwhile I'll buy Tim some driving lessons for his birthday, then, when the time comes to buy a car at least he'll be able to drive it and he can teach me later.

Her mind went into overdrive and she imagined herself dropping Sarah off at nursery school, going on to a morning job — a doctor's or hotel receptionist perhaps — then collecting her daughter and spending the afternoons at home in that lovely house and garden.

I'll go to the library and borrow some gardening books. I shan't miss the boarding house a bit, she thought. It always was a means to an end, although I did enjoy it. For most of the time anyway.

She was sorting the contents of a drawer one evening when Sarah was in bed and Tim at work, when she found an old notebook from her writing days. Squatting on the floor she started to read, and there, at the foot of one of the pages, was a note in Gordon's handwriting.

Be calm, she told herself. It was a long while ago. Yet the sight of it made her breathe faster and she felt the old excitement coursing through her body. It was only a remark about the story that was being read out. They had frequently done this if they were sitting next to each other, but for a few moments it brought back the anguish of that time — of loving Gordon without stopping loving Tim; of loving the two men in such different ways.

It wasn't just the physical chemistry of Gordon and me, she thought now, it went deeper than that. Much, much deeper. What would have happened if Gordon hadn't stayed with his wife and son? Would they have eventually found happiness together, she and Gordon and Sarah? She would never know because all the way through had been her feelings for Tim. Gentle, quiet Tim, her husband who had stuck by her through so much now.

Yet, she pondered, did you ever really know people? Never in her wildest dreams would she have imagined Tim issuing an ultimatum as he had over this coming move. Sometimes it made her shiver; because she knew that over this she would lose. He adored Sarah and she never doubted that he would carry out his threat to keep her with him.

I can understand more than ever why Gordon stayed with his marriage. His wife knew she had the trump card because of the little boy. If Tim could feel like this over a child who was not his . . . Strange how things worked out. How she had prayed for Tim to accept the baby because she loved him so much. Now it was that same little one who, unconsciously, was the pivot on whose interests most decisions were made. If it was right for Sarah then it was right for them all.

Katie snapped the book shut. This was stupid. In a moment she would be thinking that she resented her own child because of the power she had. Later, in bed, with Tim home again and fast asleep by her side, she knew she did. Just a little bit. For hadn't his first words when he came in been, 'Sarah all right?'

'Yes. Why wouldn't she be?'

'Well she had a bit of a sniffle this morning when I left and she starts her dancing class tomorrow. She'll be so disappointed if she can't go.'

18

They moved to Garice House on a wet and windy September day. Katie, usually so organized, felt chaotic as she looked around at the boxes and tea chests. She couldn't find her lists of what went where. The box containing the kettle, teapot and vital ingredients for a refreshing drink were packed onto the furniture van instead of travelling with her, and seemed to be missing.

No friendly neighbours came round. In fact she saw no one. It could have been an avenue of dead houses they were moving to judging by the eerie quietness.

Eventually some sort of order prevailed but it was late by then. Sarah was overtired and uncomfortable in a strange room. Consequently she repeatedly came downstairs every ten minutes or so on some pretext or other. Finally Katie gave up trying to sort anything that evening. Instead she took Sarah back to bed, and, because all the books were still packed, she made up a story about a little girl who moved to a beautiful house and had lots of adventures when she went to the big new school.

'Will she have some friends like Jill and Susan and Kevin to have the adventures with, Mummy?'

'Yes, darling. She'll have friends. There's lots of girls and boys at the big school.'

Eventually Sarah fell asleep and Katie returned downstairs. 'I'll get it all straightened out tomorrow, Tim. I don't know what went wrong this time. It usually goes more smoothly.'

He put his arm round her and pulled her onto the settee with him. 'The last move decided to make its presence felt darling, that's all. But we're here now, and we've found the kettle and the cups, so everything else can be done gradually. After all we have the rest of our lives.'

As his lips covered hers with kisses she thought again that she had never before witnessed Tim in such an authoritative mood. She hoped it would work out living here. It was more classy than anywhere they had been before; but she knew for certain that it had to be final or she would lose Tim and Sarah, the two people she loved most in the world. His arms tightened around her as she gave herself up to the physical pleasure of his love.

★ ★ ★

Rosedale Gardens was everything Katie wanted. Well, almost everything. It took several months to know her neighbours, but once she did they proved friendly. The houses up here were not cheek by jowl as she was used to and there was a sense of isolation, especially when Tim was at work. In those first weeks in the new house she did wonder if she had made a mistake she would have to live with forever. She had always had a knack for getting on with people from many different walks of life and this now stood her in good stead. She kept a low profile and after a few weeks she was invited to a coffee morning to discuss who was doing what at the local Autumn Fair. As the meeting progressed and several of her ideas were favourably commented on, someone said, 'You are obviously a good organizer and have done this before.'

Katie was pleased, and, smiling at the faces around the table she said, 'Well, I have been used to running my own business, I daresay that's why.'

'What line of business were you in?' the lady sitting next to her asked.

'We ran hotels,' she said.

Later, back in her own sitting room she felt ashamed at her pretence. It was dishonest to give the impression that they were four and

181

five star hotels, yet she knew this is what she had hoped to convey. She had been apprehensive that if she'd said, 'we ran a boarding house', she would have lost kudos among her new neighbours.

Tim settled well, as did Sarah. Each morning Katie took the child into town to her nursery school, then spent the intervening hours before collecting her browsing in the shops and the library and walking along the seafront. She could think more clearly if she strode along with the sound of the sea for company.

It was on one such morning that she made the decision to write a book. An historical novel, she thought. History had always fascinated her. The way people lived years ago, the way they lived in different countries, different cultures. She was interested in it all, from the eating and drinking vessels of past centuries to the furniture and architecture. It's only the people who stay the same, she thought, pausing for a few moments and leaning on the rail to watch the endless rhythm of the sea and the waves almost falling over each other and then coming to a dribble of water on the sand.

She had the time now to research her chosen period. Although at present she wasn't sure which one it would be, the thought of the exploration stimulated her. She also had access to the public library where she could check her facts.

Sarah was at the school from nine until twelve, and, apart from Wednesday when the library closed all day, Katie was oblivious for those hours to all else that went on around her.

She paused to look at the notices on the board one day, and saw that the writers' group was still operating. It seemed so long ago now, far more than six years. Occasionally, when Sarah was sitting still, perhaps painting or watching a television programme, Katie studied her features thoroughly. There was no resemblance to Gordon. The child was a small replica of her mother in all but the colour of her hair.

Sometimes too she wondered about that other baby. Was he happy? Were his parents loving and looking after him? She told herself that this was stupid, introspective thinking. It was over and done. She had known he was going to a home where he was wanted and she was only thinking about him now because she was alone so much. After the busyness of her previous life she was bound to feel a difference.

The people in the Roselands area were fine if you took things slowly. It wasn't an 'all pals together' type of place. She didn't want this, but it would have been nice if she sometimes saw someone. Many of the residents employed gardeners and au pairs and when exploring the district she usually saw more of them than of the people who lived in the houses.

Since helping to organize the very genteel Autumn Fair she had scarcely seen any of the ladies who took part; a wave as a car passed her as she walked along the road with Sarah; a 'Good morning' when she had gone to the railway station to meet John and his fiancée. That had been from a lady who lived diagonally opposite to Garice House and whom she sometimes glimpsed walking in her front garden. She often thought she would call out but always by the time she was within hailing distance there was no one there any more.

John's fiancée was called Clare and she came from Scotland. She was a wee bit nervous, she said, because John spoke so highly of them. John was impressed with the house. 'I wouldn't dare scatter my wireless bits and pieces here,' he said, laughing as they showed the happy couple over the property.

'Mr and Mrs Bray were so kind to me always,' he said, turning to Clare, 'and in each of their houses I felt it was very much my home too.' Then, to Katie and Tim, 'You

184

deserve it, you both worked so hard, and this is a very fine place.'

They had a happy weekend together. Tim was at the restaurant on Sunday and he booked them in for dinner. It was the first time for Katie and Sarah, and the little girl loved it, especially when, towards the end of the meal Clare asked her if she would like to be her bridesmaid when she and John got married the following year.

Katie watched her daughter's face as she eagerly asked them questions about the dresses, the flowers, the cake . . .

'You seem to know a lot about weddings, young lady,' John said, smiling at her, 'but remember you have a long time to wait, because it isn't until next year. But it's a promise, Sarah, you shall be Clare's bridesmaid.'

'There will be two of you,' Clare said softly, 'I have a niece who is a year older than you and, closer to the time, we will all have a get together to choose your dresses. How about that?'

They left on Sunday evening, with promises to keep in touch regularly and a very thrilled little girl finally went to bed saying, 'But I'm not a bit tired, Mummy, really I'm not.' She was asleep within five minutes.

Tim's job was a very bright spot in this new phase of their life. He was enjoying it so much.

'I always knew you would like more responsibility if you once made the break,' Katie said to him one day.

'We've changed, darling. Both of us. I wasn't ready for this years ago, but now I am. Some of your ambition must have rubbed off onto me I guess.'

She laughed. 'You said both of us, Tim. How have I changed? Am I less ambitious, do you suppose?'

He looked thoughtful, then, taking her hand in his, he said in a gentle voice, 'No, I don't think so. Maybe it's simply that you aren't as single-minded as you used to be.'

He never asked her if she was happy now she had finally achieved the top end of town. It was a question she could not yet ask herself. It will take time, she thought, yes, it will take time.

★ ★ ★

Sarah was due to begin full time schooling in September. The school she would attend was approximately half a mile from Roselands Gardens. Katie decided that she would stay at home and continue with her novel until

186

Christmas and look for a part-time job after that. She spent the last few weeks of the summer on her daughter's school clothes; shopping, knitting, sewing labels onto garments, and wishing she had another baby now Sarah would be away all day.

She dismissed the idea as quickly as it arrived each time. There was no way. Adoption was out and she must learn to be content. Given her nature she knew she needed to fill her time with outside interests once her child was attending school all day. Writing her book, her still developing interest in antiques, these would help, yet they were all passive pursuits. The guest house had been a physical one; decorating, shopping, cooking, cleaning, she had been on the go all day. Depends what sort of job I can find, she mused. It has to tie in with Sarah's school times but there's sure to be something.

Since the move she had bought one very nice Georgian table from George Pugh. Even Tim had commented on how it looked so right for the house. She loved the lounge but her favourite room was the little spare bedroom which she was transforming into a study-cum-spare room. It was small enough to be cosy, but large enough to house a single bed and chest of drawers/dressing table unit. Possibly even a desk. George Pugh was looking out for a suitable one for her.

Because of Tim's job she was alone a great deal in the evenings as well as the daytime and she was glad the garden was fairly large. It would be good to plan and plant and keep it aglow with colour and life. So far she had not had a gardener, deeming it a waste of money while she could do it herself. It would be a healthy and pleasant pursuit and give her that something physical to do that she had been thinking about. That was the secret of a happy life, Katie decided, to keep busy. Especially when things were on the change, and there was no challenge ahead.

19

Sarah was nervous the day she was to begin school.

'Will there be anyone there I know, Mummy?' she asked in a tremulous little voice.

'There may be, but you will soon make friends, darling. Remember a lot of the girls and boys will be new as well as you. So they won't know anyone there either.'

'If they have *always* lived up here they'll know each other,' Sarah said logically.

'You'll be all right, my love. Truly you will. After all, you didn't know anyone at nursery school at first, did you?'

'I knew Jill and Susan and Kevin.' Katie tried to quell the nerves in her own body as she looked at her daughter. Strange how like Tim she was in this negative attitude. Did environment have more, or at least as much, to do with the way a child behaved as genetics did? Because Gordon was as outgoing as she herself was, yet Sarah behaved the way a true child of Tim's probably would.

It was a raw morning when school began. Sarah looked pale and played about with her cornflakes instead of eating them. She fared no better with her boiled egg, which she normally enjoyed. Katie, loathe to let her go without some food in spite of her insistence that she wasn't hungry, removed the plate and gave her a packet of crisps instead. Was it always like this? she wondered. Surely the child would be all right once she was at the school. It was only fear of the unknown that was making her nervous. Or was she sickening for something? She had been to the school only two weeks previously to see the teacher, but of course, Katie had been with her. Sarah knew she would have to stay on her own now.

Because she had already been to nursery school and was used to that routine, she was to stay for lunch. Katie had packed her sandwiches and drink in the new red carrying box she was so proud of.

Sarah didn't cry or cringe around her. She simply looked sad and pale-faced. Her whole attitude was droopy. The sag of her shoulders, the sudden slowness of her walk. Katie longed to be able to say, 'Come on, we'll go for a brisk walk along the front and throw pebbles into the sea.' Instead she helped her into her coat and said as brightly as she could manage, 'Come along, time to go.'

At the school gates a group of women were

chatting. Children were racing into the playground and yelling and screaming at each other. Sarah clung to Katie's hand.

'All right, love. I'll come in with you this morning.'

A woman with a young boy smiled at her. 'The first day is always the worst for both of you,' she said quietly. 'I remember when mine started five years ago, but he loves school now.'

She turned to the fair-haired boy at her side. 'Will you look out for her at playtime, and make sure she's all right, son.'

Unhesitatingly he took hold of Sarah's hand.

'What's your name?'

'Sarah,' she said in almost a whisper.

'You'll be in the new class. The teacher's nice. She's called Miss Lupino but we all call her Miss Loopy when she's not listening. Come on, I'll show you where to go,' and then he and Sarah were walking hand in hand across the playground. Halfway over he stopped for a moment to talk to a group squatting on the ground and playing marbles. Sarah never looked back and Katie watched her tiny figure disappear inside the school door. Within seconds the bell rang and the playground miraculously emptied.

A deep sigh escaped from her and the boy's

mother said, 'I'm sure she'll be fine. But it is a wrench when they first go, isn't it? Would you like to come and have a coffee with me? My car's over there?'

'I — I think I ought to get home,' Katie said, still half expecting to see Sarah racing out of the school building towards her, 'but thank you. Another day maybe?'

'Of course. Don't worry about her. My son's only ten but he's a very caring little boy. He loves looking after people. Shouldn't wonder if he goes on to be a nurse or doctor.'

As they parted she said, 'See you tomorrow morning. My husband collects him today as it's my yoga class.'

Katie found it difficult to settle to anything during the day. She tried working on her book, but the picture of Sarah's pale face at breakfast that morning kept interrupting her. At lunchtime Tim came in. 'Couldn't get away before. How did she settle, Katie?'

'She'll — be all right, Tim. She was a bit nervous, naturally, but she made friends with a boy a bit older than herself and he seemed to be looking out for her.'

When Tim had returned to work she went into the garden. The September day which had begun so bleakly had developed into a pleasant one, warm and mellow. She was glad it would soon be time to go for Sarah.

Obviously this would be the worst day for both of them, for all three of them really; but Sarah would soon make friends at school and she would become used to not having the child around and would absorb herself in Tim and her hobbies. Their little girl was growing up. She had, after all, been going to her nursery school for three hours each morning for some time now, and Katie never remembered feeling like this about it. There had always been so much to do.

It's simply that I have absorbed some of Sarah's natural fear of a new adventure, she thought, and we haven't lived up here long enough to be part of it yet. Maybe I'll accept that invitation to coffee one morning soon, then I shall get to know the other mums.

She was at the school gates before anyone else. One or two of the women smiled at her as they arrived, some pushing prams, some pushchairs, others with a dog. Cars began to come along and soon the road was full of noise and bustle.

Sarah wasn't the first out. Katie's eyes scanned the playground, then focused on the door where even now a motley assortment of colours and bobbing heads were emerging.

Then she saw her. Walking sedately across the playground with the lad who had promised to look out for her. They weren't holding hands as they had when he took her in, but she was chattering to him and he was laughing with her. Katie felt a pang of something like pain shoot through her body; her daughter was broadening her horizons. Well, that was surely good. She need not have worried all day. Sarah was obviously integrating well. A girl who looked about Sarah's age joined them and the three of them began skipping towards the gate. When she noticed her mother Sarah waved but stayed with her new friends.

She did take Katie's hand, though, once she reached her and Katie squeezed it and sighed with relief.

'Goodbye, Sarah,' they chorused, and as the girl ran over to her mother the boy said, 'There's Daddy's car. Bye, see you tomorrow.'

A light blue car had swung into the space just vacated further along the road, and, as Katie turned to look at the man who emerged and opened the back door for his son, she felt her world spinning crazily. The man was Gordon Linnet.

Part 2

20

Thirteen years later

Katie had moved swiftly when she discovered that the little boy who had looked after Sarah on her first day at the new school was her old lover's son. Panic hit her. What was she to do? She couldn't move away from the problem this time. She knew that if she even tried to do this she would lose the two people she loved most in the world — Tim and Sarah.

Something had to be done, though, and she spent a sleepless night dreaming up various solutions. Most of them she was aware she couldn't implement. Fortunately Gordon had not seen her because she had turned away and walked quickly in the opposite direction. Sarah was so full of the things she had done she chattered all the way home and didn't seem to find it odd that she had so little response. The urgent thing, Katie thought, was to find an excuse not to meet her daughter from school on the day Gordon met his son. That was only one day a week and should be possible. She too could have a commitment on that day each week and arrange for someone else to fetch Sarah back. Not impossible. Within a week she had joined an art group which met on that day. She thought it better to have a real reason rather than a make-believe one which could easily be disproved. By the following week Katie had made an arrangement with another mother with a little girl Sarah's age, to bring the child home that day. It was surprisingly easy. She distanced herself as much as possible from Gordon's wife. She had been the first one to befriend her in this new environment but under the circumstances she must never let herself be drawn into social contact with any of the parents. Katie felt guilty about her when she remembered how she and Gordon had cheated on this woman years before. I dare not risk becoming friendly with her, though, because if I did there would be the hazard of meeting Gordon, she thought. By the same token if she accepted invitations from any of the parents there was the danger that Gordon and his wife would be there. Her only solution was to keep well out of the social scene.

Because of the five year age gap between them Katie hoped that the young lad would soon tire of having a girl tagging along. This proved to be the case as Sarah's talk became more about her friends in her own class.

Katie sometimes thought that the other parents may have labelled her snooty or difficult, but that was a price she had to pay. Upping sticks was out of the question now.

She longed to confide in Tim but knew that was out of bounds too. The hurt and damage I've caused in the past, she thought. For what? So we could enjoy the good things of life. Or what I perceived to be the good things.

With Tim at the restaurant most evenings, once Sarah was in bed Katie was thrown back on her own resources a great deal. This wasn't a problem for her — she never had been one to crave company just so that she wouldn't be alone. She had many interests: the novel she had begun writing when Sarah first went to nursery school, her garden, her growing knowledge of antiques, her love for the history of gemstones which stemmed from her short spell working with old Mr Devonshire in the little jeweller's she had loved. There was so much to be thankful for. Above all for Tim and Sarah.

She loved them both so much. She had never stopped loving Tim, even throughout her passion for Gordon. Their scraps had been clashes of personalities and almost always ended in each others' arms. Their sex life now was as good as ever — better in many ways than when they first married. They were comfortable with each other while never losing the excitement of love making. 'I think we'll still be doing this when we're ninety,' he had said the other night and that had given her a giggle as she mentally pictured them when they were old. But why not, it's only the outer person that changes shape and texture, she thought, not the thoughts and feelings inside. 'Darling Tim, I hope so,' she had murmured, kissing him.

She *had* been in love with Gordon, genuinely so, and if she and Tim hadn't been going through such a bad patch she doubted it would have taken off as it did. Yet that liaison had given her Sarah. She sometimes thought she didn't deserve all the happiness she had. Now she knew that Gordon had not, after all, moved from the area after their affair was over she was worried. He had talked about doing so and she presumed that it had happened. She never had known where he lived anyway; at the time it hadn't seemed important.

It's my problem now, she told herself. I strayed from the path and part of the payment for doing so is that now I cannot move away from the danger of that past. There was no doubt in her mind that Tim would keep Sarah if she even hinted at it. He adored the little girl as much as she did.

He had found the new restaurant fulfilling and while he didn't want to own one and have the responsibility of it as proprietor, he was a good and loyal manager. The business prospered and Tim enjoyed his work in a way he never had at the camp.

'You were right all those years ago,' he had said to her recently, 'when you urged me to try to move on. I do enjoy being my own boss but under the umbrella of someone else. I still wouldn't want the financial worry of the whole thing.

'You're happy, aren't you, Katie? You've seemed a bit quiet lately. Is everything all right?'

She had kissed him and murmured assent. He had never known the name of Sarah's father and it could do no good now to tell him of her discovery that he was still in the area and that the man's son went to the same school as Sarah. With the difference in the children's ages and gender there was no call to think they would be thrown together for any project. I am the only person who knows the truth, she thought, even Gordon didn't know he had become a father again. She did take the precaution of looking him up in the phone book, so she could avoid wandering anywhere near his house when she was out on one of her 'exploring the area' walks, but he was ex-directory. She didn't want to draw attention to herself by checking the voters list.

When she met Sarah she made a point of wandering round the area near the school but away from the main gate where the parents waited. As they brought and collected their son by car Katie reasoned that they must live some distance from the school. Probably right on the outskirts at the foot of the downs where there was some lovely property. Katie stuck to the area at the back of the school. There were some beautiful gardens to admire and when she heard the shouts and chatter of the children coming out she walked back and was always at the end of the road by the time Sarah appeared. She would wave and the little girl then ran towards her.

Katie thought she may need to invent an allergy which prevented her from mixing with other people but it hadn't proved necessary. When Sarah was nine she passed her cycle proficiency test at the school and travelled there and back under her own steam. If the weather was extremely bad, which it seldom was here on the south coast, she went on the bus. It wasn't a long journey, and although Katie was apprehensive when she was cycling she knew she had to let her go. There were no other children at the school who lived close by. Even the lady who collected her on Katie's art group day was four streets further on. Occasionally Tim would drop Sarah off at school but his work schedule didn't make this an easy option.

She did well and they both attended the school concerts and open evenings. Katie tried to keep well away from the crowds on these occasions, but as Gordon's son was obviously several grades higher than Sarah, the evenings didn't clash. In any case when the children were eleven they changed schools, and that particular danger passed. By the time Sarah had reached that stage Katie insisted she wanted her to go to an all girls school. Tim wasn't sure, but said he thought perhaps Katie was right and it was better for her — nothing to distract from her studies. Katie, who had been gearing herself up for a rare old fight should he disagree, breathed a huge sigh of relief that she didn't need to do this.

21

Tim drove Sarah to Bristol University. He didn't often have a complete day away from the restaurant although he now had an under manager who could take care of the place when he was absent. Katie went too and tried to concentrate on her pride that her daughter was actually going to university. Yet it would mean an end to the family life as they had known it for so many years now. Tim had said as much last night after they went to bed.

'Just be you and me again, like it was in the beginning,' he said as his arms came round her. 'We'll both miss her I know, but she won't be so far away and I daresay will come home for holidays.'

Katie snuggled against him, 'Yes.'

'Now we have Andy at the restaurant, we could take a winter holiday, go abroad or on a short cruise. Like the honeymoon we never had. We can afford something special now. What do you think, Katie?'

'Sounds great, Tim. Yes, let's do that. I'll go into town next week and pick up some travel brochures. Where would you like to go?'

'I'm easy, darling. Maybe somewhere with

some winter sunshine. If we plan it for early November it will escape some of our dreary weather and it's also not so busy at Suzanna's then. The summer rush is well over and the Christmas one won't be under way. I've already got plans on ice for December anyway. My staff are good and the place will run just as well while I'm away as when I'm there.'

'Because you've trained them well, my love and you treat them right.'

Over the past fourteen years since Tim had been at Suzanna's he seemed to have gained a lot of confidence in his abilities about everything. As Sarah moved through school and asked questions about her homework, which they often couldn't answer, both he and Katie began studying. Nothing drastic, but they enjoyed their free time poring over books in whatever subject Sarah was currently doing at school. Katie thought it also brought them even closer as a family. Tim had said to her one day, 'Sarah's got a good brain on her, she'll go far and we must give her every opportunity to use it. She may even go to university, Katie, something you and I never aspired to.' Katie was so proud of both of them. It set her wondering about hereditary traits and environmental ones, but she kept her thoughts on the subject to herself.

Sarah was going to read history and English and had mentioned that she might even think about teaching. She had blossomed from an attractive toddler into a tomboy child, a wilful and over the top fourteen and fifteen year old, and now, at eighteen, into a beautiful young lady. She was gentle with all creatures, and had, over the years, had rabbits, guinea pigs and hamsters. The only thing Katie drew the line on was rats and mice. 'There's plenty of other animals you can choose from but not them, Sarah, never,' she had said. Tim had laughed with Sarah when she teased her mother about them all being smaller than her and all God's creatures. Then, eyeing her sternly he had said, 'I'll add one more to your mother's list though. Snakes. Anything else will be welcome, eh, Katie?'

Yes, it had been a happy time once they had settled down as a threesome. The only niggle, which grew less as the years flew by, was the fact that Gordon and his family could still be in the area. Since that glimpse on Sarah's first day at school Katie had retreated from the social side of life of the area. Good job it happened when it did she had told herself much later, because it would have been more difficult to keep her distance had she really become acquainted with the parent set. As it was she simply never joined.

★ ★ ★

They stopped for a meal on the journey to Bristol, but didn't linger once they had Sarah and all her stuff ensconced in her room. As if reading her mother's unvoiced thoughts about the smallness of it Sarah said, rather too brightly, 'Won't be able to chuck clothes and things around in here and litter it up, will I? It will probably teach me to be tidy if nothing else.' Katie gave her two or three posters they had shopped for together the week before and, almost as if she was anxious for them to leave Sarah said, 'I'll put the posters up after you've left — it will give me something to do.' There was a definite tremor in her voice and Tim said gently but firmly, 'Good idea, Sarah. And remember, my love, all the others coming in this year will be as new as you. You're all in the same boat, so to speak. Your mum and I never had the chance to go to university, you know, and we'll be longing to hear all about it.' He hugged her then moved away as Katie buried her head against her daughter's shoulder. 'Be happy, sweetheart,' she whispered, 'love you.'

The first few weeks were lonely. Tim had

his work but Katie felt bereft. Not that Sarah had been there during the daytime of course, and she was often out with her friends in the evening, but her presence was there. Katie even missed the washing and ironing. She wrote to her a couple of times a week at first, and Sarah wrote back. Those first epistles reeked of misery. It was lonely even though there were so many students there. She hadn't made any friends at all, so many of the freshers, 'that's what the first years are called, Mum,' crowded into the bar in the evenings but she didn't like to. They spoke on the phone, but never for long. 'There's a queue here,' she reported, 'so I can't hog it.'

Two weeks into the term and it all changed. She had made friends with a girl called Sally and they had joined the drama group. The letters and calls home became less frequent and more cheerful. They had met some boys and gone with them to the cinema and to a dance . . .

With a catch in his voice Tim said, 'Our little girl has flown the nest, Katie. It's good, it's what we want for her I know, but I do miss her.'

Katie, close to tears, almost said, 'Do you think I don't?' but she stopped herself in time. 'She'll be home at Christmas time,' she said. She tried to engross herself with her writing and painting but her heart wasn't in it and she found herself remembering the ups and downs of the girl's earlier years.

Tim had been the best father ever and the three of them had had such grand times together. Some traumas too, as she grew up and thought she should have her own way over things, but nothing too drastic and Tim had backed Katie in every crisis.

'Cheer up, my love,' he said when he popped in during the middle of the day to fetch something. 'She's a young woman now. Got to lead her own life, make her own mistakes, and you've still got me, you know.'

'Oh, Tim.'

'Got to go, sweetheart, but how about coming to the restaurant tonight for a meal?'

'No, I don't think so. You'd be working and most of the time I'd be sitting alone.' He kissed her long and hard before he left and she began to worry that something might happen to him. You did read about this sort of thing sometimes. When someone is extra solicitous almost as though they know something bad is coming. He usually kissed her before he left for work, but not as passionately as that.

He rang in the middle of the afternoon. 'I've had an idea, Katie,' he said. 'How about a weekend in Bristol. We could stay in a hotel in the city and take Sarah for a meal one of the days. Do us both good and we'll be able to see for ourselves if she really is all right, won't we?'

'Oh, Tim. What a wonderful idea.' She cried when she came off the phone, cried for the sheer kindness and love her husband gave her. Cried too in relief that her worry over that lunchtime kiss had been unfounded.

It took a couple of weeks to arrange the trip to Bristol because Sarah was working hard at her studies during the day and it seemed she had a pretty full social life too. A boy's name had crept into the conversations. She had had boyfriends when she was living at home and Katie had worried then that Gordon's son might be among them. She always asked their surname, making it sound casual, but there was no one she brought indoors nor mentioned with the name of Linnet. Maybe the family had moved by now. At these times she usually uttered a little prayer that they had.

She tried not to think that if she hadn't been so keen to keep moving upwards, to always want a better house, a more comfortable way of life, then they would not have moved, albeit unwittingly, into Gordon's area. She knew that Tim had found it puzzling when she made no efforts to find chums among the other mothers of young children at the school. She had always been so sociable, such a good mixer and made friends easily. 'I've pals down in the town, and I meet up with them at least once a week, sometimes more,' she told him. 'Anyway I want to get on with writing and painting now and it absorbs all my time. I'd rather work than go to coffee mornings,' she had added for good measure.

'As long as you're happy,' was Tim's response and for once in her life she was glad of his easygoing attitudes and acceptance of her explanation. Katie's initial thought that Gordon's son would become one of Sarah's mates had faded with the years. He was several years older than her and would have moved on to senior school, possibly university, might even be married now. If the family were still living in the vicinity, and if, by an unhappy chance, they should meet somewhere socially, she was sure that both she and Gordon would cope with the situation. Although both of their spouses knew about an affair, neither knew the names or faces of the other party. She had even imagined what they would say to each other and rehearsed it to herself looking in the bedroom mirror to get her expression right as she greeted him as a new acquaintance. They were mature people now and could surely manage an encounter such as that.

She hoped and prayed it would never happen, that Gordon and his wife had now moved away, but if it did, she was prepared.

★ ★ ★

Sarah did come home for the Christmas holidays, and again the following Easter. On that occasion she brought a girl-friend with her and the two of them spent hours talking about a couple of lads they were going around with.

When they had returned to university Tim said, 'I hope she finds someone who will make her happy, someone who will be good to her, Katie. I worry about it sometimes — there are so many rotten ones in the world.'

'I found a good'un.' Katie snuggled up to him in bed, 'But I know what you're saying, darling and I pray she will too.'

'She's a sensible girl underneath all that fun,' he said, before turning to her for the real business of the night.

Sense doesn't always come into it, Katie thought as she went about her chores the following day. Sarah's father and I didn't show much sense but we did have love. Sarah was born of love. How could I have loved another man as passionately as I did, while still loving Tim? Her thoughts seldom strayed down those paths now, which was just as well, she told herself, for it did no good at all.

During the final week of the summer holidays after Sarah's third term at Bristol University she went out playing tennis every evening. She had belonged to the tennis club for a couple of years before she went to university. She classed herself a medium to good player, 'Never likely to see the inside of Wimbledon, but I really enjoy the game,' she said to Katie and Tim. 'It's good fun and they're a nice bunch of people down there.'

Sarah was out every evening for the rest of that week. On her last night her mother was not in bed when she came in. Katie noticed the ruffled hair, flushed cheeks and the happiness that shone from her daughter's eyes.

''Night, Mum,' she said, without coming further than the sitting room door, adding, 'you're up late tonight.' She had gone before Katie could do or say anything. Obviously she wasn't ready for a cosy chat and a pang of fear rippled through Katie's body.

The following day they took her to Brighton Station to catch her train to Bristol. Sarah sat in the front seat of the car next to

Tim, and, by the time they had unloaded the enormous amount of luggage the girl had with her and sorted out the platform they needed there was less than ten minutes before departure. Not the moment to start a conversation about the name of the boy who had brought that glow to her daughter's cheeks last night, Katie decided. They hugged each other tightly while Tim put her bags onto the train. Katie and Tim waved until the last carriage was out of sight, then they made their way back to the car.

Sarah rang that evening. 'The time went much too fast,' she said, 'but it was great to be home. Had a fabulous time. You two take care of yourselves and I'll see you at Christmas time. Got to go, there's a queue as usual. Love you both.'

22

Katie and Tim tried to plan another weekend in Bristol, leaving Andy Simms, the under manager, in charge. Again for late October or early November as they had the previous year, but they couldn't find a date which suited them all. Sarah herself was the one who was so busy. She had a lot of work in hand and a pretty full social life, it seemed. Tied up with lectures during the week, she wanted her weekends free she told them, 'Because there's so much going on down here and I'm out most of the time then.'

'I'm glad she's leading an independent life,' Katie said, 'and she seems to be working hard for her degree as well, so she should be able to get a good job and earn some money when she comes out.'

'Me too. I never doubted that she would work, though. She's like you, goes headlong into everything and does a thorough job. That's why your boarding houses were so successful. It's good that she's enjoying herself too. You're only young once, eh, Katie. Remember how we worked, washing up, you waitressing, me being general dogsbody at the camp, and living in that poky, damp little flat. We had a few ding-dongs over that place, didn't we?'

'Mmm.'

He adjusted his tie. 'Best get off now. Got a birthday party coming in later this evening. Fifteen of them, so that should be fun. Don't wait up dear, and I'll come in quietly.' He kissed her and then traced his finger gently over her cheek. 'I do love you, my Katie,' he said.

Sarah's next letter apologized for not being able to fit in a date for a visit from them. *I really am cramming during the week*, she wrote, *and Jon, a friend who lives and works in London during the week, comes down most weekends. Sometimes I go to London and we do a show, but he shares a small flat with a workmate and it's a bit cramped. I'll bring him to meet you at Christmas.* Her letter went on to tell them how much she was looking forward to it, and as Katie put it back into the envelope she said, 'Wonder if this is the one, Tim. She sounds pretty happy and she's bringing him home.'

'You're romancing, darling,' he said. 'Sarah's far too young to think of marriage yet.'

'Wonder if he's foreign? She's spelt Jon without the h.'

'Slip of the pen. Or it might be short for Jonathan. Youngsters shorten everything these days.'

Tim was right, Katie thought later. She felt relieved that Sarah was with someone well away from Longsands, although she didn't like the idea of them holed up together either in London or Bristol. 'It's too soon,' she said to Tim. 'She's not known him long and she's so young.'

Sarah didn't come home when the term finished. *Want to spend a few days in London, do some shows and then Sally and I are involved with a drama production here in Bristol and we have the chance to go with a group of students to France for a week after that. This has only just come up but it would be foolish not to go, I think, because it is a history tour and will be counted as part of the course. After that I'll be home. Because Jon is working he can't come with me then, but he has some leave due and will be down soon after. So it will be a few weeks before I see you but am looking forward to it as you can imagine. And I'm longing for you to meet Jon. Must dash, Sally's just come in to remind me we're going out in less than half an hour. See you, love and kisses, Sarah.*

★   ★   ★

217

Sarah looked radiant when she arrived. She flung her arms round them. 'Oh, it's wonderful to be home, and wait 'til you hear my news. Mum, Dad, I'm in love. Truly in love. I've found the man I want to marry and he's dying to meet you both. And before you say anything you don't have to worry that my education will be wasted, because we shall wait until I've graduated before we tie the knot or start a family. We want to get engaged this Christmas and be married in the church here a week or two after my graduation next year. Jon would have been here with me now but he had to go up north for a special meeting at his firm's headquarters and can't get back until late tonight, so he's coming down tomorrow. He's an accountant, did I say?' She twirled around the room. 'And I think I've done all right in my exams too. To think next year's my last at uni, it's gone so fast. I shall really work hard because I want to get a good degree. Jon got a first. There's talk of him becoming a junior partner in the firm.'

She chattered away and when Katie could get a word in she said, 'Did Jon go to Bristol too?'

'No, he was at York. Says it's a lovely city. We're going to have a long weekend up there in the spring before my studies become too intense. Oh, isn't life exciting?'

She rang some of her friends while Katie was preparing dinner and when she returned she said, 'Would you mind if I slipped out for an hour or two this afternoon? I've just been speaking to Gill and she's going on holiday tomorrow, for three weeks. I'd like to see her before she goes.'

'I have to pop into the restaurant for a few minutes to see someone this afternoon,' Tim said, 'I can drop you at her house on my way. Will save you messing about with the bus.'

'Thanks, Dad.'

It was such a happy meal. Katie gazed at her beloved daughter as she and Tim chatted and teased each other. She smiled at them both and felt a great calmness fill her being. She was glad that Sarah's boyfriend couldn't get down tonight, because it was so lovely to have the girl to themselves for a while longer. Once he was here too then doubtless the young people would be rushing about all over the place. She had made up the bed in the spare room for him although it was obvious to her that they shared a room when she stayed at his place in London.

'Come on, Sarah,' Tim called up the stairs when he was ready to go, 'I've got to meet someone in a quarter of an hour. Do you keep your Jon — is that short for Jonathan by the way — waiting like this?'

She laughed as she came down, 'Sometimes I do. Yes, it's an abbreviation of Jonathan. He says his dad usually calls him Johnnie though. I've not met his parents yet, but we're hoping to have a get together with you all this trip. He's going to ask you formally for my hand in marriage like they did in the old days, Dad.' She giggled. 'Jonathan Gordon Linnet to give him his full title, so in a couple of years' time I shall be Mrs Sarah Linnet BA. Sounds good, doesn't it? Bye, Mum,' she called out from the hall, 'I'm being rushed but I won't be too late back. I'll take my key though, in case you want to go out.'

'Bye darling, I'll be about half an hour,' Tim said.

As the door closed behind them, Katie stood up, and then raced for the downstairs loo where she was violently sick.

★   ★   ★

When Tim returned twenty-five minutes later she was sitting, white-faced on the stairs.

'Katie, whatever is it, my darling. Are you ill?' He rushed to her and she fainted into his arms.

She recovered quickly and before she lost her nerve she told him the name he had wanted to know all those years ago. 'It has to be his son,' she whispered, 'Oh God, Tim, what a mess I've made of everything.'

His arms tightened around her. 'We have to tell Sarah,' he whispered, 'if only it hadn't gone so far, but with talk of marriage it can't be halted any other way. You are sure it is — '

'Yes. He had a son and he lived in Longsands although I never knew where. Tim . . . ' Gently he cradled her in his arms.

When Sarah returned she had a photograph album in her hands. 'Gill says to say hallo to you from her. I took some pictures of Jon and me to show her. Here, meet your future son-in-law,' and she held the small book out towards them.

'Sarah, please stop, darling. There's something you need to know. There is a — a legal reason why you and Jonathan can't marry.'

'Oh he's not married or even committed to anybody else. Only to me and — '

'Sarah . . . ' Katie's voice sounded strangulated, 'Sarah, you must listen to me, it's — it's important,' she finished on a choky sob. 'You see — '

Tim said quietly, 'Let me tell her, Katie.' He put his arm protectively round his wife, and then reached out with his other hand to Sarah. 'This is going to shock and hurt you my darling,' he said, 'but remember that we love you, you are everything to both of us. But you need to know the truth and — and that is that Jonathan's father is also your father.'

She slipped her hand from his and looked at him. 'You're — you're joking, Dad. He can't be.'

'He is, my darling. Biologically he is.'

Sarah turned towards her mother. 'You mean — I'm adopted?'

'No.' The word was barely audible and the anguish in her daughter's eyes as its meaning penetrated was devastating. Her gaze flicked from one to the other as they stood close together, their hands locked into a fierce and tight embrace.

'But then — then,' the young girl's eyes suddenly filled with tears, 'Oh no, no, no, no, I don't believe it. You and Jon's dad, tell me it's not true, it can't be.' Her tear-drenched gaze darted from one to the other and then she had rushed from the room and her loud sobs and screams of agony rang through the house.

23

Tim let them in. Katie was standing in the middle of the room. 'Please sit down,' she said, gesturing toward the settee. 'Sarah's out, but she knows the truth.'

Without looking at her Gordon said, 'So does Jonathan. He was devastated. He truly loves her.'

'They're young,' Maureen said, 'They won't believe it now, but there will be someone else for them both. Surely there has to be.' The anguish in her voice was painful to hear.

It seemed unreal to Katie, that Gordon and his wife were sitting here having this discussion. She had telephoned them after Tim persuaded Sarah to give them the number. The girl refused to leave her bedroom and pushed a slip of paper beneath the door with the number written on it. He would have rung them himself but Katie said, 'No. I must do it, Tim. It's my duty.'

Her voice was a shadow of itself and afterwards she couldn't remember what she had said to Gordon, except to ask if he was sitting down. Tim stood by the telephone stool, his hands on her shoulders, ready to take over if necessary.

Now they were here, Gordon and his wife, the woman who, all those years ago outside the school, had invited her back for coffee.

Apart from a tinge of light grey in his hair Gordon looked to her as he had over twenty years ago. A few more lines maybe, but no paunch, no bald patches.

'I — I never knew your son's name,' she said, looking directly at Maureen. 'When Sarah first mentioned him it was simply someone she had recently met. I — I gather now that they've been meeting in Bristol throughout last term.'

'Go on.' The other woman's eyes were gazing at her.

'She'd mentioned Jon, said he lived in London. That they were in love and wanted to marry. Then she told us his name was Jonathan Gordon Linnet and — and — ' Katie's voice broke then as she silently recalled her daughter's next words — '*I shall be Mrs Sarah Linnet, BA.*'

Maureen had her hand on Gordon's arm, almost as if she thought he might go over to his former lover to comfort her in her distress. He turned to look at his wife. 'I swear I never knew about the baby, Maureen.'

'I believe you,' she said, then to Katie,

224

'How can you be sure that Sarah is my husband's child? I accept you had an affair with him, but — '

'Then accept that Sarah is biologically his,' Tim's voice as he broke in was raw with emotion. 'Do you think we would put either of them through this if it wasn't true? She is your husband's child but I am her father. I have brought her up as my daughter. In every other way Sarah is my daughter. My name is on her birth certificate.'

Tears welled in his eyes and Gordon said quietly, 'Whichever way you look at it, it's a mess and two young innocents are suffering. But if I am Sarah's father and also Jonathan's father we cannot allow them to marry.'

Katie had gathered herself together and now she looked at him and said solemnly, 'You are, Gordon. There's no doubt about that.'

With a definite tremble in her voice Maureen said, 'Jonathan is certainly Gordon's son, but as we are being so frank with each other, and we do need to be with our children's future at stake, I will tell you something we have not told another living soul.'

Katie held her breath and Tim gently squeezed her hand. 'I did not carry him myself. I could not, but we wanted a child so much that another woman acted as surrogate for me. But he's my son. Mine and Gordon's.'

Into the silence Katie whispered, 'Not through an agency in Paddington that was about to close down?'

The two women stared at each other while both men looked bewildered for a few seconds. Maureen was the first to speak. 'No, no, it can't be. I don't believe it. I *won't* believe it.' Fumbling for her handkerchief she whispered, 'Bilton and Bognor.'

Katie nodded. She had no words left. Into the agony of silence the telephone shrilled an escape for them. For two or three seconds no one moved, then Tim walked across the room and picked up the receiver.

Sarah's voice was heard clearly through the instrument, 'Come quickly, Jon's shut himself in his bedroom and I don't know what he's going to do. Hurry, oh please hurry . . . '

They went in Maureen and Gordon's car which was parked in the drive. The urgency in her voice stopped them wasting time getting their own from the garage.

It was a fifteen minute's drive to the outskirts of the town, and as the car screeched to a stop the four of them tumbled out, leaving all the car doors wide open.

Katie saw Gordon's hand shaking as he

fumbled with the key and Maureen snatched it from him and unlocked the door. 'In there,' she snapped to them, and then she ran up the stairs, leaving the rest of them in the sitting room.

They could hear her talking to her son, 'Jonathan, open the door, *please*. We can work this out. Just let me in. Come on, my darling, it's not as bad as you think. Open the door and we'll talk, there *is* a solution I promise you.' Katie could hear Sarah's voice too, but it was so soft she couldn't make out what she was saying. She longed to go up there and cuddle her daughter, try to make it better as she used to when she was a little girl but in this situation there was nothing she could do to stop her hurting. There was no way she could make anything better for her now. Tim was clinging tightly to her hand, whether to stop her or himself from moving she didn't know, but suddenly the entreaties from upstairs stopped and there was the faint sound of a door opening and closing.

Suddenly she was aware that Tim was speaking to her, 'come on, darling, let's find Sarah and take her home.' Without looking round she rose and let her husband lead her into the hall. A white-faced Sarah was coming down the stairs, holding tightly to the bannister like an old lady afraid of missing her step. Gordon came from the sitting room, went to the front door and led the way down the path, 'I'll run you back,' he said, 'you can't walk all that way.' His voice sounded flat, expressionless, and he never looked directly at any of them. Sarah sat in the back with her mother and Tim in the passenger seat next to Gordon.

The girl scarcely moved as Katie's arm went round her shoulder. She sat there, ramrod straight, cold as ice, her face set like a mask. When Gordon stopped the car outside their house, Tim was first out. He opened the back door, took Sarah's hand and walked with her up the path to the front door. She was like a zombie. Katie clambered out and saw Gordon watching Sarah with moist eyes. He turned his gaze onto her and for a couple of seconds their eyes spoke to each other and she saw her own pain reflected in his. Then he brushed his hand across as if to wipe out the visions he was seeing. Without speaking he got back into the car and drove away.

★   ★   ★

Sarah went to her room and refused all efforts to make her come downstairs for anything. The cup of coffee Katie took up was still outside the door an hour later. 'Just leave me alone, I've things to do,' she said, adding more gently, 'Don't worry, I shan't do anything silly.'

The next morning she came downstairs, puffy-faced and red-eyed. She played about with some cornflakes and a cup of tea, then disappeared back to her room.

Tim had organized for Andy, his under manager to be at the restaurant for the lunches but neither he nor Katie were able to coax Sarah into leaving her bedroom.

'We must give it time,' Tim said.

'It's all my fault. I love her so much. I love you so much and I messed everything up. I wish I were dead.'

'Don't start talking like that, Katie. She'll need you later on and I need you now. We have to be strong for her. She needs a while to come to terms with everything. It's been a tremendous shock for her.'

Tim went to work in the evening and Sarah appeared to be asleep when Katie looked in. She had eaten one of the two cheese sandwiches which Katie had taken upstairs for her earlier. The empty plate left outside the bedroom door with just the crusts left on, as she used to when she was little, told its own story.

They both whispered 'goodnight,' when Tim came home and they went to bed. She didn't answer but they heard the curtains being pulled and Tim gently edged Katie towards their own room.

'She's okay,' he whispered.

There were no sounds from her room at breakfast time. 'She must be exhausted,' Katie said, 'we'll let her sleep, shall we?'

Katie tapped on her daughter's bedroom door about eleven that morning and when there was no reply she opened the door and went in. The bed was neatly made but there was no one in the room. Panic hit her as she gazed round, half expecting to find her beloved child lying dead somewhere on the floor, but the place was devoid of humanity. She rushed into the bathroom but that too was empty. A strangled sound came from her lips as she returned to Sarah's room and it was then she saw the purple envelope lying on the pillow.

Katie sank onto the bed because suddenly her legs didn't feel as though they could support her. She didn't know whether to open it or to rush out and look for her daughter. A flicker of logic shot through her and she picked up the envelope and extracted a single sheet of paper. *Dear Mum and Dad*, it read, *I can't say much. I'm too full of things. I'm going away for a bit. I won't go back to uni, I shall travel around Europe and* sort myself out. Jon and I decided this yesterday just before you arrived. He had had the offer of a job in Africa for two years. He was going to turn it down, but now he will accept it. I know I shall never stop loving him and I also know it can't be for us. I'm not blaming you but I don't want to be with you at the moment. I've got my savings book and my passport and I shall work my passage. I don't hate you. Every part of me is numb, even my feelings for Jon. I'll be in touch. Sarah.

24

Fourteen months later Sarah arrived home. There had been a postcard from Germany ten weeks after she left. *I am well*, it read, *and seeing quite a bit of Europe. Sarah.*

There were three more after that, well spaced out and all from different places. The most recent one was from Florence. *The architecture here is wonderful and so are the art galleries. Have done some painting. Love Sarah.*

Katie and Tim read and re-read them all so many times. 'She's put love on those last two,' Katie said, 'if only we had an address we could write back. Or a phone number — or — or something.'

'She'll be home one day,' Tim said. 'It's amazing what the human heart can cope with, given time.'

Katie remembered vividly how Tim had coped and how he had come to love Sarah so much when she herself was in hospital. It was the turning point for him, but would Sarah ever again be the loving daughter she had been before? Or did a deeply ingrained love go on in spite of everything? She asked herself these questions but she couldn't bring herself to discuss them with Tim.

Eight months after the young people had left there was a phone call from Gordon. She had answered it while Tim was watching the news on the television.

'Just to tell you that we are moving,' he said. 'I'm going to manage the firm's Scottish branch. Have you heard anything from Sarah?'

'A few postcards,' she answered quietly. 'She's working in Europe.'

'We had a letter from Jonathan last month.'

'I'm glad.'

'Sarah's a lovely girl, Katie.'

There was silence, possibly only for a few seconds but it seemed to her it was a long time. Then they both spoke at once.

'Well, it was really to let you know our plans,' he said.

'Thank you, and Jon sounds a nice lad. Under other circumstances . . . '

'I know.' His voice sounded hoarse. 'Goodbye, Katie.'

'Goodbye, Gordon.'

She told Tim and he said, 'Best thing that could happen. Because she will be back some day you know. I'm sure of it. I dream of her sometimes and she's always here with us in my dream.'

'That last card was the best one yet,' Katie said, 'but I'm afraid to hope too much.'

★　★　★

It was just after eleven o'clock on a Sunday morning when Tim came into Katie's study. 'I'm off then, dear, be back about four I expect. How's it going?' He indicated the mass of papers spread over her desk.

She pulled a face, 'Not well. I can't seem to get this chapter right. I've redone it so many times. I might just leave it and do some gardening instead this morning. I can't seem to settle at all. Maybe the book's no good anyway and that's why I'm stuck.'

'Nonsense, darling. It's just a bad patch. An hour in the garden, a cup of coffee and you'll come back and sail through it.'

'You reckon?'

'I do.' He leant over and kissed her. 'Must get off. We're fully booked this lunchtime. See you later, sweetheart.'

As he turned to go, the doorbell chimed. 'I'll get it on my way out. We aren't expecting anyone, are we?'

Katie stood up. 'No.' At the back of her mind was always this vision that one day Sarah would come home. That she would open the door and there she'd be. It was

234

something she had not voiced to Tim because she knew without him saying so that it was his dream too. The bell seldom rang unless it was expected. It was not the sort of area that attracted cold callers and there was no post on a Sunday. Tim's delighted gasp, 'Sarah . . . ' floated like magic up the stairs. She felt goosebumps tremble throughout her body and she almost tumbled down the last three stairs in her haste to reach the door.

At first she didn't notice the man with her daughter. They simply fell into each others' arms, and she was oblivious to everything except the fact that Sarah was home. It was Sarah who drew her companion forward saying, 'This is Guiseppe. We've been together for seven months now.' Smiling lovingly at him she said, 'Darling, this is my mum and dad.'

'I am very pleased to meet you,' he said, as though he had been rehearsing the line. He leaned towards them, and kissed first Katie, and then, to his embarrassment, Tim, on both cheeks. Sarah laughed, 'Oh Dad, if you could only see your expression. It's an old Italian custom you know. Well do we get to come in or have we to stay out here all day? We're both hungry and parched — it's been a long journey.'

The door was opened to its full extent,

235

and, hand in hand, they stepped inside. Sarah inhaled deeply and her eyes misted over. 'It smells just like home.' she said.

Katie felt Tim's hand on her shoulder as they led the way indoors. Too full for words she turned her face towards him and although her eyes were awash with tears, her smile was radiant.

We do hope that you have enjoyed reading this large print book.

Did you know that all of our titles are available for purchase?

We publish a wide range of high quality large print books including:
Romances, Mysteries, Classics
General Fiction
Non Fiction and Westerns

Special interest titles available in large print are:
The Little Oxford Dictionary
Music Book
Song Book
Hymn Book
Service Book

Also available from us courtesy of Oxford University Press:
Young Readers' Dictionary
(large print edition)
Young Readers' Thesaurus
(large print edition)

For further information or a free brochure, please contact us at:
Ulverscroft Large Print Books Ltd.,
The Green, Bradgate Road, Anstey,
Leicester, LE7 7FU, England.
Tel: (00 44) 0116 236 4325
Fax: (00 44) 0116 234 0205

Other titles published by
The House of Ulverscroft:

SCRIPT FOR MURDER

Joan M. Moules

It's 1955. In the seaside town of
Fairbourne, on the south coast of
England, is the Victoriana theatre. One of
the actors has been murdered in his
dressing room at a time between the
matinee and the evening performance.
Everyone working in the theatre falls
under suspicion, especially the cast and
the murdered man's wife, who is more
famous than her husband. Inspector
Carding and Sergeant George Binns
investigate, whilst the actors, used to
playing a part, suspect one another. Yet to
leave before the season finishes will point
the finger at the murderer . . .

CROSS MY PALM

Sara Stockbridge

London, 1860s. High society ladies enjoy having their fortunes read whilst attending supper parties. But palm reading is a perilous business: the lines of the left hand can unlock secrets best kept hidden. Entertaining the guests of Lady Quayle at Portland Place, fortune-teller Miss Rose Lee reads Emily's palm. 'A quiet life, my dear' is what she tells the girl. But she spies two little crosses that spell something quite different — fearful, violent death. As Rose's predictions start coming true, her own fortunes become embroiled in the suspect fates of others and the future suddenly seems a dark and dangerous place.

THE TENDERLOIN

John Butler

It's 1995.Embarking on an adventure, Evan lands in San Francisco from Dublin with his friend, Milo. The city is on the cusp of a revolution: the Internet is booming, whilst the rave scene succeeds the old world of Deadheads dropping acid on Haight Street. He finally lands a job at ForwardSlash — a new dot com company — run by the charismatic Sam Couples, a surrogate father figure, yet the object of confused emotions for the naive Evan. Life begins to look up — until Milo's ex-girlfriend arrives, reminding him of their own brief encounter and dragging the past over with her.